Chante
Wilhelm
Made in Germany

CW00507500

Chantecoq, Volume 2

Arthur Bernède

Translated by Andrew K. Lawston

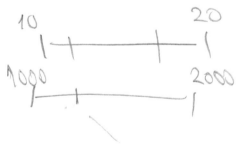

DEDICATION

For Melanie, and for Buscemi, the Kitten of Detectives.

Proof copy – corrected after
audio recording in August 2023

A. Lawton

17/09/23

CONTENTS

ACKNOWLEDGMENTS

This book was translated from *L'Espionne de Guillaume* by Arthur Bernède, first serialised by *Le Petit Parisien* in 1914.

The cover design was by Rachel Lawston of www.lawstondesign.com.

1 COMPLETE MYSTERY

Monsieur Mazurier, Minister of War, feverishly paced his huge office on Rue Saint-Dominique. He was about fifty years old, his hair and moustache greying, his eye shining and energetic behind the eyeglass perched on his proud nose, his forehead creased by a worried frown.

Monsieur Servières, Director of Sûreté générale[1], a man of around forty years, dressed in a black redingote coat whose lapel was decorated with a red rosette, and sitting in an armchair, facing a huge desk piled with files and documents of all sorts, observed him with an air that was both serious, and saddened.

Turning suddenly towards the powerful civil servant, the Minister cried in a tone full of nervous impatience, "So be it. What's your advice?"

---

[1] *Sûreté générale* - a French civilian agency responsible for public safety and enforcement, which also inherited certain counterintelligence functions in the aftermath of the Dreyfus Affair in 1899.

"I feel," replied Monsieur Servières, "that we find ourselves in the midst of a serious conspiracy organised against our national defence..."

"So, what do we do?"

"Act quickly, but with the greatest secrecy. Consider for a moment, Minister, the emotion which would rise up among the people if the newspapers published that our arsenals might explode one after the other like simple champagne corks, and our artillery shatter as easily as an electric bulb!"

"It's frightening," declared Monsieur Mazucrier, chewing his lip. "Ah! How to stop this work of destruction, how to discover the wretches who are its authors? These people are very strong."

"Very strong indeed," acknowledged the Director of the Sûreté, "and I know of only one man capable of trapping them."

"This Chantecoq you've been telling me about?"

"Precisely, Minister."

"He's one of your best bloodhounds?"

"He's better! Chantecoq is both a character and an intelligence. He has performed immense services for us, in France and abroad... You will certainly have heard talk of the Germaine Aubry affair?"

"That young French governess who, having gone to Germany to recapture documents stolen from her father, was arrested and condemned as a spy to twenty years of fortress imprisonment?"

"Quite. It's thanks to Chantecoq that she was able to escape and return to France."

"I remember, indeed..."

"That's not all, Minister. This admirable detective also succeeded in capturing the infamous Emma Lückner, the most fearsome of all German spies, who uncovered so many of our secrets and caused so much chaos among us."

"Wasn't that the ragamuffin," asked the Minister, "who was condemned to ten years of solitary confinement?"

"That's her," confirmed Monsieur Servières, "transferred to the central house in Rennes, she died after six months in any case, after taking a dose of poison she'd managed to procure for herself - we never found out how."

"From what you're telling me," continued the Minister of War, "this Chantecoq is the most valuable of agents."

"Beyond compare. He's not only gifted with a flair which makes him the most skilled policeman I know, but he has pushed to the art of camouflaging himself, of transforming himself, of making himself unrecognisable in a few moments, to its very limit. By turns an officer, gentleman, peasant, worker, priest, magistrate, bourgeois, speaking several languages with the same fluency and without any accent, rejuvenating and ageing himself at will, growing and shrinking according to his whims, he is the definitive Protean man.

"Added to which, he's gifted with indomitable courage and an athletic vigour which permits him to keep up with the most formidable adversaries…"

"It's admirable!" the Minister exclaimed. "And has he been in your service for a long time?"

"Chantecoq has never been officially attached to Sûreté générale. He works when he pleases, as a dilettante."

"That's strange! And you're sure of him?"

"As sure as I am of myself."

"In that case, my dear Monsieur Servières, I'd be very grateful if you could send him to my office straight away."

11

The Director of the Sûreté, taking out his watch, said simply, after consulting it with a rapid glance, "Chantecoq ought to be here now, Minister. Anticipating that you would want to speak to him, I told him to arrive at the Ministry of War on the stroke of four. It is now two minutes to four; and as he makes a principle of always arriving five minutes early, I'm sure he's already been waiting for you for three minutes. Will you allow me to go and check?"

"Be my guest, Director."

Monsieur Servières stood, went to the door which led to the antechamber, opened it a crack, and immediately spotted, sitting peacefully on a bench, a man in the full prime of his life, and whose elegantly sober attire, fine face, and attractive appearance announced a perfect gentleman.

"Chantecoq," said Monsieur Servières, "The Minister of War will see you now."

The detective stood and, to the great astonishment of the hussars who hadn't dared to intervene, he strode directly into the Minister's office.

"Monsieur Chantecoq," began Monsieur Mazurier, "Sûreté's Director has been singing your praises to me. Doubtless he has brought you up to speed on the events which led to your presence in my office?"

"No, Minister," replied Chantecoq in a calm and assured voice. "Monsieur Servières simply told me that France had need of me, so here I am."

While speaking this sentence, the bloodhound raised his head, his gaze steadily meeting that of the Minister, who suddenly discovered there such energy, depth, and intelligence, that he welcomed him in a tone full the keenest interest.

"Sit down, Monsieur, and let's discuss the matter! I'm going to confide in you a state secret. For some time, confidential reports have made me aware that a certain number of German spies have infiltrated France with the clear goal of destroying our resources, burning our arsenals, and blowing up our fortresses.

"Some catastrophes have already occurred. Now, you perhaps aren't aware that Germany is currently making preparations for war with prodigious activity."

At these words, Chantecoq gave a simple movement of his head which seemed to say, "I know."

The Minister of War continued. "If a conflict broke out tomorrow - heaven forbid - as a result of these machinations whose origins I can only suspect, we would find ourselves, from the point of view of armaments and the quality of munitions, in a disastrously inferior position!"

"The scoundrels!" Chantecoq growled between his teeth.

Monsieur Mazurier explained. "I must tell you that we've already discovered some very interesting details. In particular, I have a report from the chief engineer of powders and saltpetre, who concludes very simply that the danger resides in a malfunction of flash cotton made by our gunpowder mill in Douai.

"But, where things become extremely troubling is that the Director of the Douai gunpowder mill, Colonel Richard, is not only an officer whose ardent patriotism must serve to place him above all suspicion, but a genius of the first order who has rendered us the greatest services.

"I'll even add that I entrusted him with the fabrication of a new explosive Z1, something formidable, invented by the famous Jean Aubry, to whom we already owe the Combat Aircraft[2]. So, you'll understand… I'm trembling!"

The Minister fell silent, choked with emotion.

Chantecoq, after a moment of silence, replied in a reflective and serious tone. "There's certainly a traitor in the house!"

"It's that very traitor," cried Monsieur Mazurier, "that I'm asking you to unmask!"

"Ah well, I'll certainly try, Minister!"

"When are you leaving for Douai?"

"Tomorrow morning, because I need to familiarise myself with the file."

"All my documents are at your disposal," said the Minister.

"As are mine," added the Director of Sûreté générale.

"One simple question, Minister," continued Chantecoq.

"Go on..."

"Is Colonel Richard aware of all this?"

"No," Monsieur Mazurier replied curtly. "It's only the Director of the Sûreté, you, and myself who know the truth."

"In that case, Minister, I'll be able to act with a free hand."

And Chantecoq, his eyes shining, his head held high, declared in a satisfied voice. "It's interesting, very interesting. Can I just confirm we're agreed that I'll have *carte blanche* in this matter?"

"Absolutely."

"Then everything's splendid!"

"So," asked the Minister, "you hope to discover the culprits?"

"I can do better than just hope, Minister," the detective replied, "I'm sure of it."

"And soon?"

[2] See *Chantecoq and the Aubry Affair*

"I can't give you a date…" And with an air that was both mysterious and knowing, Chantecoq added, "All I can tell you, Minister, is that I'll 'collar them'. I give you my word of honour."

2 IN THE COUNTRYSIDE

It was five in the evening. The June sun was still casting its warm rays on the road from Arras to Douai.

A beggar, his face tanned, despite the shade provided by a filthy old felt hat, a grey messenger's bag over his left shoulder and a stout knotted staff in his right hand, was advancing by dragging his leg, slowing his pace every so often in order to look behind him.

Soon, as though he was overcome by fatigue, he stopped completely, put his bag on the ground, sat at the edge of the ditch by the side of the road... then, after being assured by a suspicious glance all around that he was completely alone, he began to murmur. "Now, I'm ready... I can begin the manoeuvre!"

Then, standing again, instead of following the road, the tramp climbed the bank, crept through the hedge on top of it, and set off on a narrow path which led straight across the fields and which seemed to give him access to a vast factory whose buildings and chimneys could be seen in the distance.

In this manner, the stranger reached a small wood which had grown up at the bottom of the small valley, when, suddenly, he froze, one ear to the winds, his eyes darting about, his nostrils flared.

He had just noticed, heading towards him, a man of about thirty years, dark brown hair, his upper lip surmounted by a dashing moustache, with a military bearing beneath his civilian suit, and a gaze full of deep and reflective intelligence.

"Lieutenant Vallier!" the tramp muttered, and added immediately. "Hold on, hold on! What's he doing coming this way at such an hour?"

With disconcerting ease, the man with the courier's bag disappeared instantly behind a tree, in order to fall to the ground and immediately take on the air of a drunk who would be deeply asleep for some time yet.

The newcomer, who seemed to be very absorbed, passed by without noticing him. As he moved away, the officer let out a cry. "Yvonne!"

A young girl, quite tall but attractive and charming in her precocious robustness, her radiant complexion, her clear eyes, her mouth half-open in a smile which was not without a certain note of melancholy, had burst from a small clearing that was bathed in discreet light, and advanced towards the Lieutenant.

"Yvonne!" repeated the young man with an accent of bottomless fervour.

"Raymond!" said the exquisite creature in her turn, holding her hands out to him chastely.

And straight away she declared, "You must have been surprised, shocked even, when I wrote to you, to ask you to come and meet me here?"

"No!" said the Lieutenant. "I simply felt in my heart a sensation which was both painful and very tender…"

"Then you still love me?"

"Yes, I love you!"

"Then why do you want to leave?"

"Who told you that?" said Vallier with a start.

"It doesn't matter… I know you requested a transfer and it pained me," replied the young girl, her eyes full of tears.

"Listen, Yvonne," replied Raymond, "and I'm sure you'll understand and approve of my actions."

While keeping hold of the young girl's hands, the young man continued.

"It's one year since I had the audacity to request your hand in marriage from your father. He refused. I know perfectly well that I possess nothing other than my salary in terms of a fortune. I have my old mother to care for. Notwithstanding, I was so insistent that, very cordially, Colonel Richard said to me, 'Let's hear no more of this, let's never speak of it again. I value you highly, and it would cost me dearly if I was forced to deprive myself of your services.'

"I therefore held my tongue to obey my commanding officer, but above all in order to remain near to you, to see you. And I was almost happy, because if our lips remained mute, our eyes could at least speak, and said enough for us both to be certain we still loved each other."

"And then?" the young girl asked softly.

"Three days ago, I heard Colonel Richard say loudly to one of his friends who happened to be in his office: 'I believe I've found a good match for Yvonne… a rich industrialist from Maubeuge, Monsieur Louis Marois. I've not yet spoken of the matter to the girl, but I hope that won't cause her any difficulty.'"

"And you doubted me?"

"No, Yvonne, but I thought I had no right to complicate - what am I saying - to perhaps ruin your life… and I preferred to take off, to disappear and to leave you at liberty."

"That liberty, Raymond, I refuse it. I'll marry no one other than you."

"In spite of your father's wishes?"

"My father's wishes, I can bend in your favour. I'll manage that, I'm sure of it. If my poor mother was still alive, I'm certain we would already be together."

"But you'll have to struggle…"

"I *will* struggle and I will vanquish!"

"My beloved," said the young officer, bringing Yvonne's delicate white fingers to his lips.

"So you're going to stay put," continued Colonel Richard's daughter. "Our eyes will continue to say very tender things, our hearts will continue to beat as one, our souls to love, awaiting the blessed hour, which I'm sure won't be far away, when my father consents to our marriage! But you will not leave!"

"No, I won't leave," Lieutenant Vallier murmured simply.

After exchanging a long look full of promises and love, the lovers parted.

He vanished among the trees. She returned to her parental home, situated in the very interior of the Douai powder mill, on the edge of the town.

As to the tramp, he slowly pulled himself up onto his hands and knees, then, his eyes glittering with mischief beneath his bushy brows, he muttered through his teeth, "My dear Chantecoq, I think it's time to make Colonel Richard's acquaintance."

3 TRAGIC ENIGMA

Colonel Richard, a man of medium height, but robust, with a florid complexion and a thick white moustache, was sitting at his desk, signing numerous administrative documents which were his responsibility, when a young orderly came in, presenting his superior with a card. He took it and read, printed in light but clear characters, the simple name: *DALIBERT - State Engineer.*

"I don't know him!" said the Colonel, surprised and hesitant.

Chantecoq, transformed into an immaculate civil servant, aged and respectable, was already standing in the doorway, and said in a detached tone, "Colonel, I beg your pardon for intruding in this manner. But I know that you dine at seven. It's only six o'clock, so we have time to talk."

While the orderly hurriedly retreated to the corridor, closing the door behind him, Monsieur Richard stood, his attitude cold, displeased, and asked in a haughty tone, "Ah! Monsieur, who are you, to take it upon yourself to -"

Ever imperturbable, the detective interrupted him. "Are we alone, Colonel?"

"Yes, indeed."

"And you're certain no one can hear us?"

Then, fixing his steely gaze in Colonel Richard's eyes, the French detective told him everything.

"I've been sent on a mission by the Minister of War, and I've come to warn you that there's a traitor at work here!"

The Colonel jumped. "A traitor? Here!"

"Yes, Colonel!" Chantecoq affirmed with the greatest calm.

And slowly drawing a folded piece of paper from his jacket pocket, he said, "Please familiarise yourself with this report from the engineer in charge of powders and saltpetre."

Nervously, Yvonne's father took the document. As he scanned it, his face seemed to collapse.

When he had finished, in the grip of a terrible shock, he let himself fall into his armchair while murmuring in a strangled voice, "That's abominable!"

Then, while fat tears sprang from his eyes, Colonel Richard shouted. "No, no, the more I think about it, the more I tell myself that this is absurd, impossible! To expose the country to the worst catastrophes... Let's see... Monsieur... Leaving aside the fact I maintain the most rigorous surveillance over operations... only Lieutenant Vallier and myself are aware of the secrets entrusted to us. I don't suppose you've done us the atrocious injury of suspecting us?"

"Oh! Colonel," the policeman protested with an accent of the greatest sincerity, "I know you are honour itself. As to Lieutenant Vallier..."

"He's a boy for whom I will answer."

"Permit me, however, to ask you a few questions about him?"

"Speak, Monsieur, I'm listening."

The policeman replied, hiding with difficulty the emotion which was troubling him. "Lieutenant Vallier has only his salary on which to live, doesn't he?"

"Yes, Monsieur."

"Doesn't he have any family responsibilities?"

"His old mother."

"One year ago, Colonel - pardon me for starting with these little details, but they are necessary - one year ago, didn't you refuse him permission for your daughter's hand?"

"That's right."

"Because he was poor?"

"And because, having no fortune myself, I didn't want my daughter to know hardships…"

"That's it, all right," said Chantecoq, as though speaking to himself.

"So!" cried the Colonel, pale with anguish. "You believe Lieutenant Vallier could be guilty of such an odious crime? To sell out his country! Him, a French officer!"

"Didn't you just tell me," riposted the detective, "that only you and he are fully informed?"

"I repeat, Monsieur," the Colonel cut in energetically, "that to accuse this Lieutenant is to insult me personally."

"I'm not accusing," Chantecoq interrupted in his turn, "I'm seeking to understand. One more question, Colonel. Isn't it the case that Lieutenant Vallier recently requested a transfer?"

"It's true."

"Good…"

"What do you conclude from this?"

"I conclude nothing, Colonel. One last question? Do you employ many civilian workers at the powder mill?"

"A very small number. Anyway, they're all former junior officers who possessed the best references. Furthermore, they don't know. They can't know. I tell you again, it's only Vallier and myself… It's abominable! Abominable! The more I think about it, the more I ask myself… Vallier, he… that would be so dreadful… and yet…!"

Stricken, Colonel Richard took his head in his hands, murmuring in a broken sob, "A French officer! I can't believe that. I can't believe it!"

Then, recovering suddenly, he pressed his hand on the button of a buzzer placed on his desk.

Chantecoq stopped him, saying, "What are you doing?"

"I'm going to call Lieutenant Vallier."

"Take great care, Colonel!"

"Why?"

"Because if he is indeed guilty, we must at all costs avoid alerting him."

And Chantecoq went on. "Tomorrow morning, around nine, I shall return to your office, you'll introduce me to the Lieutenant. But you will do so calmly, and prudently. It's vital not to arouse the enemy's suspicions in the slightest."

"In your view, the enemy is Vallier, then?" the Colonel asked.

"Ah… Um…" the policeman gestured evasively.

Inflamed with indignation, Monsieur Richard cried. "Ah! If it is, I think I'll strangle him with my bare hands! When I think that tomorrow I was going to give him the formula for the new Explosive Z that Jean Aubry recently invented…"

"I was going to speak to you about that precise matter."

23

"Think what a disaster… that secret delivered to the enemy… exploited against us…"

"You're absolutely sure, at least, that no one is aware of that document?"

"Absolutely sure. Since I received it, it has not left my safe for a single moment."

"Very well, but it mustn't be left in there," said the detective, throwing a suspicious glower at the furnishing in question.

"What should I do? Keep it on me?"

"Does Jean Aubry have its copy?"

"Deposited in the offices of the Ministry of War."

"In that case," decided Chantecoq, "there's not a moment to lose. You'll do me the favour of burning that immediately."

"You're right, it's the safest course," the Colonel agreed, walking towards the safe, while the fake Dalibert, already quite at home, was lighting a candle placed on the chimney.

Monsieur Richard returned, the document in his hand.

The policeman seized the paper, brought it close to the flame: then, watching it being consumed into cinders, he spoke in a mocking tone. "At least that's one explosive with which those bandits won't be waging war on us!"

But he had hardly uttered this when a colossal detonation shook the whole building, breaking the windows and making all the furnishings tremble.

The two men hurried to the window, in time to see in the gathering darkness an immense blossom of flames which, darting like an arrow, shot into the sky like a dreadful fireworks explosion.

"Good God," cried the Colonel, "that's Douai's artillery park, it just exploded."

For a moment, Monsieur Richard remained frozen as though struck by vertigo. Then, gathering himself, he called in a strained voice. "Monsieur Dalibert."

Chantecoq had vanished.

4 COLONEL RICHARD

"So… is it true, Colonel, that the park exploded?" Monsieur Richard, who was returning with a furrowed brow to the house in which he lived within the powder mill, was asked by a worker of a certain age, but with a squarely athletic build and with a gaze full of energetic tenacity.

"Alas! Yes, it's only too true, my brave Gerfaut," replied the commanding officer who appeared preoccupied.

"All the same, it's too much," replied the worker, who had been employed for several years as night watchman at the Douai powder mill. And he added in the most wrathful tone. "To think this is the third park to explode in three months. The one at Verdun, the other at Givet, and now this one! It's certain there's some treachery behind it. Ah! The brigands! They deserve to be exterminated to the last man!"

The Colonel said, while clapping the guard on the shoulder, "You're right, my brave Gerfaut. Such scoundrels aren't worthy of pity. In the meantime, double your vigilance."

"You can count on me!"

"Goodnight, Gerfaut."

"Goodnight, Colonel."

While the worker disappeared into the night, the Colonel arrived home.

Looking worried, his daughter was waiting for him in the doorway.

"Father! There you are at last!" she cried joyfully.

"Were you worried?" said the officer, kissing her forehead.

"It's half-past eight…"

"I wanted to visit the scene of the accident."

"Yes, ah well?"

"It's terrible! Eight batteries blown to smithereens… and at least twenty-five victims. It's appalling!"

Noticing her father's shocked face, Yvonne took his arm and said in a very soft voice, "Father, calm yourself… Come in, please!"

Docile, the Colonel followed his daughter who led him gently to the dining room. On the table, their old maid Françoise had put out a steaming tureen from which drifted the appetising odour of a country stew.

Heavily, as though asleep, the senior officer fell into his chair and, his head between his hands, he murmured, "Our poor young soldiers, our brave artillery men!"

"Papa, I beg you, don't get in such a state," begged the young girl, putting her arms gently around her father.

And with a voice full of tender inflections, she added, while planting a gentle kiss on the industrialist's forehead, "It's still not your fault!"

"Yes, you're right, it's not my fault, it's not my fault!"

Françoise, who had entered discreetly, also offered her advice in a trembling voice. "You must eat your soup, Colonel; if not it will go cold."

The officer remained as though in a daze, his arms dangling, his gaze vacant.

Without any sound, Yvonne filled her plate, asking herself, "What's the matter with him, my God, what's wrong?"

The meal continued.

Monsieur Richard remained silent, holding back his tears with great difficulty.

When Françoise went to fetch the roast, Yvonne couldn't bear it any longer. She stood and turned to her father, saying: "You're worrying about something you don't want to tell me about."

"No, not at all."

"Oh yes, I'm sure of it. The explosion is a tragedy. But there's something else, I'm guessing. As you think I resemble my poor mother so closely, why don't you confide your troubles in me as you would have confided in her?"

"You really want me to tell you…"

"Yes, yes, yes, I'd like…"

"No, no, it's impossible, impossible!"

Françoise reappeared, a letter in her hand, and announced, anxious, fearful, as though she was breathing a cursed atmosphere. "The orderly just brought this! He said a gentleman he didn't know sent this for you and said that it was pressing, very pressing…"

"Very well. Give it to me."

While the maid was returning to her kitchen, Monsieur Richard tore the envelope and read what followed:

Colonel

Would you like to discover the man who betrayed you? Very well, come and meet me at the Chapelle de Saint-Nicolas at once…

A friend.

It goes without saying to recommend that you exercise the most absolute discretion.

On reading this unexpected missive, the officer's attitude was suddenly transformed.

Now, a flame of hope shone in his eyes. His face regained its usual colour. His hands trembled no more, because he was thinking:

"There's no doubt, this is from Monsieur Dalibert. Let's go!"

And it was almost with a cry of joy that he said, "Here's some good news, my little one. But I must leave immediately…"

"You're not finishing your dinner!"

"No. This is very urgent, my dear. Give me a kiss. Let it be enough for you to know that I'm happy, very happy. Good evening, and goodnight, my child."

"Goodnight, father!"

"What's all that about?" Yvonne thought, struck in her turn with a vague anxiety.

***

At a rapid and alert pace, the Colonel left his lodgings, to set off on the Lille road.

Becoming preoccupied again, he fretted. "Just so long as Monsieur Dalibert isn't about to reveal to me that Lieutenant Vallier's a traitor! I don't think I could stop myself from boiling his head! But why would he have committed such a dreadful crime?

"For money? To be avenged on me... who refused Yvonne's hand? And that transfer he solicited. Was he afraid of being discovered? What an anguishing enigma! And how eager I am to learn the truth..."

The Colonel was about to set off on the path leading to the Chapelle Saint-Nicolas, an old ruined sanctuary, lost in the middle of the fields, when a voice rang out in the night.

"Colonel."

Monsieur Richard turned.

Lieutenant Vallier stood before him.

"Excuse me, Colonel," began the officer, with an embarrassed air. "I saw you traveling this road... I took the liberty of joining you. Because I've something very serious to tell you and I prefer not to wait until tomorrow."

"What is it?" the powder mill's director asked severely.

"Colonel," replied Raymond in an oppressed voice, "I beg you, if there's still time, to cancel my transfer request."

At these words, Yvonne's father had shivered; but, contenting himself, he replied more coldly. "I shall see..."

Then, immediately, with no transition, he asked in a brusque tone, "Do you have any news about the artillery park explosion?"

"I'm returning from Douai right now; the general opinion is that we're dealing with an act of espionage."

"Ah! They're saying that?"

"Yes, Colonel."

"Your opinion?"

"It seems very possible."

"Very well. Good evening, Vallier," said the Colonel.

And, as he set off on the path which led to his rendezvous, he said in a voice which was rough and devoid of all benevolence, "Come to my office tomorrow, around nine o'clock. I have to put you in touch with a State Engineer, Monsieur Dalibert, on a matter of business."

"Very well, Colonel."

Already his superior officer had disappeared into the night.

"Yvonne has high hopes," Vallier said to himself, "that man will never give me his daughter's hand."

In the grip of a nervous depression which was all too understandable, the Lieutenant lay down on a bank and, his head in his hands, he began to dream.

As for Monsieur Richard, he continued his journey at an ever-increasing pace, so eager was he to have the key to the mystery, so ardently did he yearn to banish the horrible suspicions which were beginning to overwhelm him.

He took barely quarter of an hour to cross the twelve hundred metres separating the powder mill from the chapel.

Enormous stormy clouds, behind which the moon's wan disc was shining, allowed rare stars to be seen here and there among the gaps.

The Colonel approached the ruins.

Behind the door to the private wing, he spotted or rather glimpsed a shadow, while a voice that he believed he recognised called out in a lightly mocking tone.

"You're punctual, Colonel... to the very minute!"

Yvonne's father stepped forward, a little disconcerted but without hesitation, because he was brave.

Then he made out on the porch's threshold... a man dressed as a worker and who, taking two steps towards him, asked in the same ironic tone, "Well, Colonel, don't you recognise me?"

"Gerfaut!" the powder mill's director exclaimed, overcome with surprise!

"The very same, Colonel."

"What are you doing here?"

"I'm going to tell you, Colonel…"

And, pointing to the old sanctuary, which looked tragic in the night, he added: "Let's go in there, we'll be better able to talk."

All the time wondering what these preliminaries could possibly mean, the commanding officer followed his night watchman, in whom he had complete faith. In this way they arrived in the middle of the chapel.

Gerfaut began brusquely. "Just now you received an anonymous letter summoning you here?"

"How do you know?"

"I wrote it!"

"You?"

"Yes, me."

Then, in a curt voice, imprinted with a decisive, authoritative tone that his boss didn't recognise, Gerfaut, whose gaze shone with a mysterious light, declared: "The Minister of War recently entrusted you with the formula for a new explosive. Bring this formula to me, in one hour, and one hour only, and there's a million for you…"

And while the Colonel remained struck in a stupor, the wretch added in a more mocking tone, "That will do your young lady no harm at all, especially as she has no dowry!"

But Gerfaut said no more. In a furious rage, Richard threw himself on the man, claiming, "Ah! So who are you then to dare to offer me such a deal? Me? Colonel Richard!"

Gerfaut answered only with a diabolical sneer.

"How!" roared the officer. "You... the model worker, you who were recommended by the most honourable people!"

And, seeking to marshal his disturbed wits, Yvonne's father continued. "In that letter which you didn't dare sign, you promised to bring me face to face with the man who betrayed me."

"Ah well!" the false worker drawled cynically, "I've kept that promise."

"Wretch!" the Colonel started. "So you're the traitor who ruined everything here! It's you who, all while feigning devotion and patriotism, accomplished this most nefarious trick. You represent the gang of German spies unleashed upon my country! And I who was accusing the unfortunate Vallier! Ah! Wretch, you played your role well! And now you want to make an accomplice of me? Me, an old soldier, ready to die for his country! Don't you know who you're dealing with?"

And jumping on Gerfaut's throat, the commanding officer, whose strength was increased tenfold by rage, yelled. "Now I've got you, bandit, and I'll not let you go!"

Hardly had the unfortunate man proffered this phrase than two detonations echoed under the vaults of the old chapel: and the Colonel, struck in the neck by two bullets, collapsed, struck down on the slabs, while several shadows emerged from behind the pillars and, silently, advanced towards the body lying on the ground.

Then Gerfaut, leaning over his victim, began to rummage through the unfortunate officer's pockets, while snarling through gritted teeth.

"Der Teufel! How we are going to serve him, to France!"

5 WILHELM'S SPY

Madame Férel was an odd creature who, some months ago, had come to open a shop for "Curiosities and Objets d'art" on Rue Faidherbe in Lille.

Tall, thin, angular, her face wrinkled like parchment; her eyes hidden beneath black lenses that she never removed because, she claimed, threatened by cataracts, she didn't want to be operated on at any cost; her hair was grey, still thick enough, but imprisoned under a lace bonnet such as old ladies wore during the Second Empire. She hadn't taken long, thanks to the softness of her speech, and the amenity of her manners and the regularity of her payments, to win her neighbours' esteem, her suppliers' confidence, and even a certain clientele.

A true air of mystery and legend formed around her quickly.

It was rumoured that Madame Férel was hiding her illustrious origins behind an assumed name and that, an authentic marquise or countess, she must have had to, following a change in fortunes, resign herself, under the guise of a dealer in antiquities, to gradually liquidating the vestiges of her opulence along with her last remaining family souvenirs.

Others recounted that she was simply the skilful representative of one of those manufacturers of ancient trinkets, such as exist in Paris and who open up branches in all France's towns, to help their products flow.

One detail that might have supported this last hypothesis was the coming and going, infrequent but clearly noticed, of individuals bearing every mark of those bric-a-brac seekers who are so common in the countryside, and who are commonly called "chinas".

In spite of these little gossips, the widow Férel, who knew how to generate sufficient business to allow her to honour her commitments, enjoyed, following the traditional cliché, general respect.

Every evening at eight o'clock, she closed the shutters of her shopfront, lifted the latch on the door, drew the interior bolt, turned the key in the lock and, after depositing the day's takings and her most precious trinkets in a coffer at the back of the shop, the area which served as both her dining room and bedroom, she prepared a modest meal for herself.

Doubtless she went to bed soon afterwards; because, from nine o'clock, no passerby ever saw any ray of light shine beneath the door or through the shutters.

That evening, after attending to her usual routine, widow Férel, having finished her dinner which was composed simply of a mug of bouillon and a chunk of cold meat, sat in an old Louis XV chair and plunged in a deep reverie, from time to time consulting the old upright Picardy clock in the corner of her room.

When ten o'clock chimed, she stood, and headed quietly towards a door which led to an alley, behind the house.

She listened first, then opened the door, poked her head outside, looked around and waited.

"Nothing," she said, "it's curious that he's still not there. Did the mission fail? And yet, every precaution was taken."

Slowly she closed the door again, returned to her dining room, tidied away her dishes in a cupboard; and, as she looked again at the clock which marked quarter past ten, two blows, struck in a certain fashion on the door to the alley, made her raise her head.

"This time," she murmured, "it's him!"

With a quick, decisive pace, which was not that of an old woman, she went to open the door.

An individual of tall stature, of substantial corpulence, and who had every appearance of a comfortable industrialist or merchant, was waiting in the doorway.

On seeing him, the antiques dealer could not hold back a start of astonishment.

"Marois!" she said simply.

"Yes, yes," the visitor replied in a curt voice.

"Come in!"

Madame Férel stepped aside to let in the stranger who, as a man aware of the gossip about the house, wasted no time in entering the dining room, where the old lady, after carefully relocking the door, went to join him.

Then in a brief, authoritative voice, she asked, in German this time: "Ah! What business brings you here this evening?"

And without waiting for a response, she added immediately, "You know very well that I don't like to be disturbed at short notice."

"I have two pieces of good news for you."

"Couldn't you have asked for an appointment?"

"No. Because there are urgent decisions to take."

"Very well. Speak!"

While removing his coat and his hat, Marois, whose blue eyes were slightly sunk in his face, with round coloured cheeks, and a mouth surmounted by a blond moustache trimmed in the American style, seemed to radiate complete self-satisfaction, began to speak, still in the dialect from across the Rhine.

"I've finished purchasing the land overlooking the Mauberge forts."

"Ah! Finally!" Madame Férel cut in with an expression of visible joy.

"In eight days we'll be able to begin work," Then, lowering his voice, Marois added, "and in six weeks at the most, all our points having been spotted, it will only remain to establish the concrete carriages - ready to receive our siege cannons…"

"Captain Ulrich von Herfeld," the spy intoned gravely, "you have done well by the Emperor and by the German people."

"That's not all," continued the fake industrialist, whose face took on an even prouder expression, "Two days ago, in Douai itself, I had a long meeting with Colonel Richard."

"And what was the result?"

"He almost granted me his daughter's hand," Ulrich revealed, beaming.

"Too late…" the adventuress cut in.

"What? Too late?" the Teutonic officer exclaimed, his grin freezing instantly on his lips.

"That business has dragged on too long," continued Madame Férel implacably, having resumed her imperious cutting tone.

"I couldn't have gone any faster."

"Possibly. But I received urgent orders. The military staff in Berlin needed Jean Aubry's formula within forty-eight hours. I had to hurry things along, at all costs… I acted."

"And you succeeded?"

"I'm confident that in the next few minutes, I'll be in possession of the precious document."

"Permit me to doubt that."

"Why?"

"Certainly, it's been five years since, under the name of Gerfaut, Colonel von Reitzer successfully infiltrated the Douai powder mill. He's done some good, even excellent work.

"But I doubt that, despite all his intelligence and audacity, he's managed to get his hands on such a secret. The French have been good enough not to be suspicious, however everything has its limits. This will put a brake on Cannon 75. We need it for our expenses and our pains. We'll need more time, a lot of time, too much time, while I… once I'm in the Colonel's family…"

"As deeply in love with his daughter as you are," interrupted the antiques dealer in a trenchant voice, "you wouldn't take long to get sloppy, and perhaps even forget yourself!"

"Never…" protested the German, whose gaze began suddenly to shine with a fierce light.

"In the meantime," ordered the spy, "this project of a union must be renounced."

"And yet…"

"That's my decision."

"And if von Reitzer should fail?"

"He will succeed."

"You're sure of that?"

"Absolutely sure."

"Well, we shall have to see!"

"Yes, that's what we will see!"

Hardly had Madame Férel uttered this phrase when a sharp whistle echoed in the alley.

"Here he is!" cried the spy, whose eyes glowed with a strange flame.

And she hurried towards the door.

6 COLONEL VON REITZER

A few seconds later, the adventuress returned to the back of the shop with Gerfaut.

On seeing the worker, Monsieur Marois, in one movement, straightened up, automatically adopting a military attitude.

"Good evening, Captain," the newcomer said to him laconically, in a flat voice.

"Sir," replied the other without hesitation.

Gerfaut, heavily, fell into a wicker chair.

Then, poorly disguising the anger which seemed to have seized her, the antiques dealer said, in a tone shaking with ironic anger, "So! I see it's still missing."

"Yes," repeated Gerfaut, or rather Colonel von Reitzer, "yes, it's still missing."

Madame Férel shrugged her shoulders pointedly. Then, in a curt, high voice, she ordered, eyeing the officer-spy who still seemed more crushed by discouragement rather than fatigue. "Speak!"

"I was certain," revealed von Reitzer, "that Colonel Richard held Jean Aubry's formula hidden in his safe. In accordance with your instructions, I resolved to hurry things along... and acted the following night.

"My plan was quite simple. I was in possession of the safe's combination. It therefore only remained to fracture the lock, but I thought, given the mechanism's complexity and solidity, that this operation would have required too much time and above all risked making too much noise.

"So I resolved to simplify things, drawing Richard into an ambush, killing him, and seizing the key, which never left him, I was equally certain of that."

"And so?" Madame Férel punctuated in a febrile voice.

Von Reitzer continued. "I carried out my plan, just as I described it. I succeeded in luring my man to an old isolated chapel...

"Two of our men were hidden behind pillars. At first, I tried corruption, but I was wasting my time there. Those people... they aren't traitors!"

"Confound it!" sighed the spy, with an impatient gesture.

"I particularly wanted to enrage him," the German officer reflected with an accent of unspeakable hatred. "And I succeeded. If you'd seen the fury with which he attacked me. He had a solid grip, the animal... I thought he was going to strangle me. But my men, whom I had posted behind the pillars, opened fire. He collapsed to the ground. I seized his wallet, his key... I returned to the powder mill... I opened the coffers... I looked... looked... and I found nothing. Jean Aubry's formula was no longer there."

"Ah, this is too much!" the spy cried, stamping on the floor violently. "I believed you to be better than all this!"

While an indefinable smile wandered across von Herfeld's lips and while Gerfaut, dominated entirely by the mysterious and terrible widow Madame Férel, maintained the most profound silence, Wilhelm's William's spy continued.

"This is stupid… nonsense… ridiculous! So much effort to lead to such a deplorable result! Without counting the disastrous consequences that this useless murder might have for us."

"Be assured!" Von Reitzer declared, "We took precautions. Richard's body has been so well hidden that I'd defy anyone to discover it. And even if this eventuality does come to pass, it won't be us that are accused, I swear to you."

"In the meantime, we still don't have the formula," Madame Férel huffed. "And yet… Colonel, you weren't mistaken. It really was in the safe?"

"That same morning, I saw, saw with my own eyes, Colonel Richard put it in there carefully!"

"So he took it out again, during that day," continued the antiques dealer, as though speaking to herself. "He must have had an extremely serious motive… perhaps he was warned."

"I owe it to the truth to tell you," replied von Reitzer, "that from certain words uttered by Richard in the Chapelle Saint-Nicolas, I realised he was aware of 'leaks' originating from the powder mill, and that he even suspected Lieutenant Vallier."

"You see!" the adventuress was becoming even more irritated. "You must have committed some imprudence, some gaffe!"

"And yet I assure you…"

"This is going really badly!" lamented the wretch who, nevertheless, tried to master her nerves as she continued. "How to clear all this up? Wait! Did Richard have any visitors during the day?"

"I wouldn't know what to tell you, there. I left the powder mill very early. I was resting in the afternoon, and I only returned in the evening, after the explosion at the artillery park."

"You must learn more of this matter!"

"It will be done!"

"Ah! I'm furious. What do we tell Berlin? I committed absolutely, and I always keep my word. I must have that formula. Yes, I must have it, in eight days, do you hear me, Colonel, eight days!"

Suddenly, as though she'd just been struck by a brilliant idea, the spy cried. "No! Thinking about it, there is a way. It's the only way in any case… go back to the source."

And with a voice full of superior authority, the spy decreed: "Colonel von Reitzer, this formula that you didn't manage to discover in Richard's safe… it's with its inventor. Go to Jean Aubry to recover it."

"To Jean Aubry!" the officer repeated as he leapt to his feet, while Captain von Herfeld's smile grew.

"Yes, to Jean Aubry!" the adventuress insisted in a tone which brooked no reply.

"Are you joking?" the Teutonic soldier was almost babbling.

"I never joke," riposted the implacable Madame Férel. "I'm telling you, and I'm repeating, that it's Jean Aubry to whom you must go."

"No one goes to Jean Aubry any more."

"Why?"

"Indeed, you know very well…"

"I know that since a German officer by the name of Wilhelm Ansbach succeeded in infiltrating the man's home, gaining his confidence and robbing him of the plans for his combat aircraft - which his daughter was able to destroy before the Chief of Staff in Berlin used them - yes, I know this inventor has been surrounded by all sorts of precautions and that he's been forced to render his documents inaccessible to those who would like to seize them from him.

"His house in Saint-Mandé has become a true fortress. His laboratory is defended by a formidable electrical network, with an ingenious mechanism which only he can activate.

"Anyone unwise enough to trespass on Aubry's home risks, it appears, being instantly blasted."

"And you want me to go there!"

"You'll go! You'll go!" the spy repeated with a tone that underlined her prodigious will.

Then, she carried on, giving her voice a less rigorous tone. "I'm going to give you, however, the means to enter Jean Aubry's home without risking the slightest danger."

"I'm curious to know…"

"It's very simple… You're going to resuscitate Richard."

"Resuscitate Richard! How so?"

"That's to say, you're going to put yourself in his skin, or rather make him live again in yours."

"You can't be thinking of that!"

"On the contrary, I'm thinking of nothing else."

"This can't be serious!"

"It's inspired!"

"If I understand correctly, you want me to imitate his head, that…"

"Nothing would be easier for you. Not only are you of his height, of his age and his strength, but you lived near him for several years, you've been able to observe his features, his language, his habits, his ticks and his quirks. You know his private life, right down to its most hidden details."

"That's true!"

"Skillful as you've become, under my direction, in the art of disguising yourself, it would be easy for you to create a Colonel Richard which will completely fool Jean Aubry, who I happen to know has only seen him two or three times in any case. Once in place, you only have to maneuver.

"I won't tell you any more. I'll simply add: this must be done, Colonel von Reitzer, for the Emperor, and for the glory of Germany!"

"I'm ready to obey you," declared Gerfaut, whose mind seemed to be completely decided by this supreme abjuration. "However, will you permit me a word?"

"Speak!"

"Don't you worry that my departure, coinciding with the disappearance of Colonel Richard might not provoke astonishment which could easily, in the probable event that my absence will be prolonged, transform into suspicion?"

Once more the spy shrugged, then she spoke. "It happens from time to time that you fall ill."

"Not often… but however…"

"You will be ill again… for as long as necessary."

Then without any kind of transition, she asked, "Did you come here by motorcycle?"

"Yes."

"Very well, return to Douai quickly. Hide yourself. Take what you need. You know potion no. 4 well… give yourself a good fever tomorrow morning. Summon a doctor, he'll prescribe eight days of bed rest. It's up to you to set the stage for your little scene, to appear holed up at home. That's child's play, especially for a man of your skill and your calibre!

"So, goodbye, Colonel, and remember, you hold Germany's destiny in your hands."

"I shall do my duty," von Reitzer replied simply, and after bowing respectfully to Madame Férel, he left, serious, worried, almost tragic, barely responding to the military salute that the fake Maubeuge industrialist gave him.

The spy and von Herfeld remained alone together.

Both were quiet.

She, her forehead creased, upright, immobile, appeared to be plunged in deep reflection.

He, from a corner of the room, watched her with strange attention, visibly anxious, tormented…

Suddenly, the adventuress's curt voice rang out. "Captain Ulrich," she said, still authoritative.

"Madame?"

"I've just made an important decision."

"I'm listening!" replied the German officer, with the same prompt attitude as if he had been standing before his General.

Then, walking towards him, the antique dealer put her hand on his shoulder, and spoke slowly, weighing her words.

"I've changed my mind, Captain Herfeld. In one month, you must have married Colonel Richard's daughter!"

7 IN ANGUISH

Just as she did every morning, as soon as she was dressed, Yvonne knocked at her father's door to wish him a tender good morning.

How surprised she was to observe that instead of the affectionate '*enter*' which always welcomed her, she was greeted by the most profound silence.

She tried again.

There was no response.

Remembering that she had gone to sleep before having heard the Colonel come home, she thought, "Doubtless father stayed out late. I'll let him sleep."

After an hour, overcome by sadness, she returned and knocked again.

Still nothing!

So she gently pushed on the latch and quietly, on tiptoes, she entered the bedroom whose closed curtains left it still in semi-darkness.

While she headed towards the window, she murmured in a voice full of soothing inflections. "Father, I'm sorry for waking you; but it's nearly ten o'clock. You'd scold me if I let you sleep too late."

With a graceful gesture, she raised the curtains to let light flood into the room.

A painful cry burst from her chest.

The bed was empty and hadn't been slept in.

"My God!" she said, frozen in anguish.

But, recovering at once, she pressed an electric buzzer next to the chimney.

A few moments later, Françoise, the chambermaid, came running.

Noticing the bewildered face of the young mistress whom she had raised and whom she loved as though she were her own child, the brave girl cried out. "What is it, Mademoiselle, you're all pale, and trembling?"

"Françoise," replied Yvonne, "my father didn't come home."

"Not come home! What are you saying? He never goes out in the evening. It's not possible!"

"Look!" the pretty girl said simply, pointing the bed out to Françoise, who exclaimed at once, "My word, it's true! What could have happened?"

Clinging to an idea, which was quite reasonable after all, the old servant added, "Perhaps he stayed late to work in his office? He has so much work at the moment."

"However," replied Yvonne, "he would have returned this morning, if only to kiss me."

"If Mademoiselle wanted to go and see, all the same… that way, you'll be certain."

"You're right, Françoise. Wait for me, I'll be back shortly."

Her heart gripped by a sorrowful presentiment, Yvonne quickly crossed the blossoming garden which lay before the house, which was situated inside the powder mill itself. She crossed the courtyard, went straight to the red brick building which looked cold and severe, entered a corridor and knocked on a brown door on which was fixed a card decorated with two little tricolor flags, in the middle of which were printed these words in round handwriting: *Colonel's Office*.

Febrile, impatient, nervous, the young girl didn't wait for an answer before entering.

"It's me, father," she called out in a faint voice.

But she stopped at once.

There were indeed two people in the room.

One was Lieutenant Vallier.

The other, a middle-aged man, to whom a long greying beard, and an impeccable black frock coat, decorated with the red ribbon of the Légion d'honneur, lent the most respectable air.

"I beg your pardon, gentlemen," Mademoiselle Richard was already apologising, "but I came to see if the Colonel…"

She stopped, choked with emotion.

Lieutenant Vallier declared hurriedly, "We're waiting for him ourselves, Mademoiselle."

And pointing to the stranger, who had stood at the sight of the young girl and bowed with the most distinguished manners, the young man added, "The Colonel had an appointment this morning, at nine o'clock, with Monsieur

Dalibert, State Engineer, and I was about to send someone to remind him."

"My father isn't at home," Mademoiselle Richard blurted out.

Incapable of controlling the sorrow that was oppressing her any longer, she fell into a chair, revealing, almost in tears, "He didn't come home last night."

At those words, while Monsieur Dalibert couldn't disguise a start of surprise, the Lieutenant, running to Yvonne, cried out in the grip of visible emotion, "Mademoiselle, what are you saying? The Colonel…"

"Didn't come home," repeated the young girl, whose eyes were full of huge tears. And she managed to finish, broken, "Something terrible must certainly have happened to him."

"Don't think such a thing, Mademoiselle," advised the engineer. "Perhaps the Colonel, following the artillery park explosion, was summoned by the military authorities, as a matter of urgency."

"My father would not have left without warning me," replied Yvonne. "And then… and then..."

She fell silent, as though the words had been left hanging at the bottom of her throat.

"Speak, Mademoiselle," Lieutenant Vallier prompted her gently.

"Yes, speak!" Monsieur Dalibert insisted too, having also approached her.

Calling on all her energy, Yvonne replied. "Yesterday evening, at the house, something happened which I didn't think was very important at the time, but which, now, may throw some light on father's mysterious disappearance."

"Ah!" muttered the State Engineer, who seemed most intrigued.

The Colonel's daughter continued. "Father came home extremely saddened by that catastrophe which claimed several of our soldiers' lives. He hadn't been so down, so painfully afflicted, since my poor mother's death. I tried to lift his spirits, but in vain... when, suddenly, he was brought a letter which he read at once. Then his face lit up, and he said, 'There's some great news!'

"And without even taking the trouble to finish his dinner which he'd hardly touched anyway, he left after kissing me goodbye. I've not seen him since!"

"That's unbelievable!" said Lieutenant Vallier, who was gazing with eyes full of chaste tenderness and ardent compassion at the pretty girl whose tears were flowing, slowly, sadly.

She continued in a halting, sobbing voice. "I don't know anymore. I thought maybe he was here... I clung to that hope! And you're also waiting for him! Some misfortune must have befallen him! My poor father! He's so good! So generous, so brave! It's dreadful."

"Calm yourself," the Lieutenant tried to comfort her. "All is not lost, it's certainly just a misunderstanding. The Colonel would have charged someone with letting you know. That task wasn't carried out. These things happen in life. You mustn't torment yourself. The Colonel will certainly return."

"No! No!" Yvonne declared. "I've a premonition that I'll never see him again... he's left forever!"

"Mademoiselle," Monsieur Dalibert intervened with a note of paternal kindness. "Trust me, you mustn't despair like this."

With a persuasive tone, both consoling and designed to inspire confidence, he continued. "Will you permit me to ask you a few questions?"

"Go ahead, Monsieur," the poor child responded feebly.

"You just told us a letter was brought to your father, in the middle of dinner."

"Yes, Monsieur."

"Who brought this letter to the Colonel?"

"The chambermaid."

"Where did she get it?"

"From a messenger."

"And the messenger?"

"From someone, he said, whom he didn't know."

"Good. That letter as you already told me, caused Monsieur Richard a keen pleasure?"

"Very keen."

"He didn't tell you what it contained?"

"No, Monsieur."

"What time did he leave?"

"I couldn't tell you precisely. It was between nine o'clock and half past nine."

"I can be more precise," declared Lieutenant Vallier.

"Ah! Really!" Monsieur Dalibert exclaimed.

"Indeed, I met the Colonel around two hundred metres from home, on the Lille road. It was precisely nine-fifteen."

"On the Lille road, you say?" observed the State Engineer, more and more interested.

"Yes, Monsieur. I exchanged a few words with the Colonel who, indeed, gave me an appointment for this morning in this office, where I was to meet you. Then, he walked away…"

"Did you notice in which direction?"

"I believe, but I'm not absolutely sure, that the colonel might have turned off down a small path which leads to a ruined chapel. Chapelle Saint-Nicolas, that's what it's called, isn't it, Mademoiselle Yvonne?"

"Yes, Lieutenant."

Monsieur Dalibert, still precise and tactful, continued to ask questions, addressing the officer. "You weren't surprised to meet Monsieur Richard in that place and at such a late hour?"

"I thought," replied the artillery officer, "that Colonel Richard, after the emotions stirred in him by the explosion at the park, felt the need to take some air. It was a very fine evening…"

"Forgive me, Lieutenant, for asking you for one further piece of information, but then I'll finish."

"Speak, Monsieur, please."

"Was your meeting with the Colonel fortuitous?"

Raymond Vallier spoke with the most complete frankness. "No, Monsieur. I had a personal, private matter to communicate to the Colonel. I was returning home, when I saw him walking away down the road. I followed him, caught up with him."

"Thank you!" Monsieur Dalibert interrupted, and his manners might have appeared to those less troubled than Mademoiselle Richard and the Lieutenant to be rather more like those of a prosecutor than those of an engineer.

But Yvonne, in whom this stranger seemed to inspire one of those spontaneous confidences which can only be explained by an instinctive, sudden, irresistible fondness, cried out, raising her trembling hands to him.

"Oh! Monsieur, Monsieur, you who seem to be so kind, since you're taking such an interest in my poor father's fate, advise us, tell us what we ought to do?"

"Perhaps we ought to warn the General commanding the army corps?" Lieutenant Vallier suggested.

"Or the district attorney?" Yvonne offered.

Monsieur Dalibert did not reply at once.

He reflected, carefully, seriously, like an experienced, cautious man, who does not take decisions lightly.

Then, after a few moments, he said, "No! We mustn't do anything rash! It's wiser to wait for a day or two, because all is not lost… far from it! Leave it to me."

And in an enigmatic tone, full of assurance, the engineer added, "I've some personal connections which will allow me to conduct a swift and discreet enquiry, which will certainly be finished before long."

"Oh! Monsieur, how grateful I am to you!" Yvonne cried. "If, thanks to you, I might be able to find my dear father!"

"All I can promise you, Mademoiselle," replied Monsieur Dalibert, "is that I'll do the impossible in order to uncover the truth. But, in the meantime, I must ask you to remain silent. You, Mademoiselle, hide your anxiety, and your sorrow.

"You, Lieutenant, appear as calm and assured as usual. If you're asked where the Colonel is, simply reply that he's away on a trip. I'm asking you for forty-eight hours of patience. If, once this time has expired, I've learned nothing, we'll adopt a different approach. Count on me."

"Thank you again, Monsieur."

"Courage, Mademoiselle."

Monsieur Dalibert withdrew, after clasping Yvonne's hand affectionately.

Lieutenant Vallier accompanied him to the office door.

"Monsieur," said the officer, "though I've only had the honour of your acquaintance for a few minutes, allow me to tell you how much confidence you inspire in me too."

"I hope to prove myself worthy of it," said the engineer simply, slipping outside.

When the door closed again, a cry, or rather a sob rang out. "Raymond!"

Broken, miserable, Yvonne tried to take a few steps towards the young officer.

As she staggered, Vallier caught her in his arms.

Won over by the sobs of the adorable girl, who nobly, chastely and sublimely trusting, clung to him, he murmured, "Yvonne, I love you!"

8 THE CHAPELLE SAINT-NICOLAS

A worker, dressed in large velvet trousers and a black coat, wearing a battered hat and with a face bristling with a black and wiry beard, was following the steep-sided path which led from the Lille road to the Chapelle Saint-Nicolas.

From time to time, he turned back furtively, slowing his steps, then resumed his course, all while mumbling some unintelligible words.

He arrived in front of the ruined sanctuary, stopped, looked around, as if he wanted to check he hadn't been followed, and then he muttered, "The path ends in this cul-de-sac. So this is where the Colonel came. He can't have gone any further. Let's have a look!"

Chantecoq began with a slow tour of the chapel, examining each corner, using a ~~tree~~ branch that he'd picked up to push back the nettles and scrub which were growing along the walls.

He couldn't have discovered anything interesting, because he soon decided to pass through the crumbling old porch…

It was broad daylight.

The sun shone through the holes in the roof and the side windows had long been deprived of stained glass. They were garnished simply with rusty iron bars that were poised to detach themselves from the granite where they had been embedded for centuries.

The detective murmured, "A truly dramatic setting. Curious, this old carved wooden altar…"

Approaching, he climbed the three steps of worm-eaten wood in order to admire the altar's details, the work of an unknown artist.

"Very good, the tabernacle, beautiful sculptures. It's curious that an antique dealer didn't think to buy it or take it away."

But suddenly, like a hunting dog scenting prey, Chantecoq cried out, "Hello! What's this?"

The detective had noticed, on the tabernacle door, in the middle of a quite finely sculpted chalice, a round black hole which seemed to have been made quite recently, because splinters of fresh wood could be seen all around the orifice.

"Here's some wood," he grumbled, "which has been bored by more than just worms!"

Then, arming himself with a knife whose blade was extremely fine and pointed, he inserted the tip in the opening, and applied light pressure.

Almost instantly a dull sound rang out, while a heavy round object fell on to the altar.

The detective seized it and, raising it to his eyes between his thumb and index finger, he identified it with a satisfied smile. "A revolver bullet! By Jove! I knew it! It was here that Richard was murdered. But what could they have achieved by that?"

57

After stowing the revelatory bullet in his wallet, Chantecoq went down the steps and, standing in the middle of the chapel, he looked around in a slow circle, looking for a reference point to continue his investigations.

After a minute, nudging his foot on the dark slabs which decorated the floor, the detective, his face shining, decreed, "He's under there!"

Then, bending down, Chantecoq began to crawl on his knees, striking each stone with the hilt of his knife and reaching in this way a larger slab where one could barely read some inscriptions which were almost erased by the passage of time and feet.

"The Saint's tomb!" he said still between his teeth. "Is there any chance they would have dared profane such a place? After all, when one murders a man, one is already close to sacrilege."

But suddenly, a cry escaped Chantecoq in spite of himself. "Blood!"

Indeed, some dried and blackened drops were visible on the ground, in the shimmering sun.

Immediately, the policeman concluded, "This fresh dust, this light notch, also quite fresh, ~~and which~~ must have been made by a pick… or a lever, I'm following it by Jove! He's there! He's there! Very good, my old Chantecoq, congratulations… you're truly on form, today!"

Fast and agile, the bloodhound went to one of the windows, tore off one of the rusty bars with one twist of his hand, returned to the tomb and, placing the end of the iron in the notch he'd just discovered, he forced up the funerary slab which shook, slipped, revealing an excavation, at the bottom of which, lying on his back, was the corpse of Colonel Richard.

"It's him! It's really him," the detective recognised the man immediately. "That's another blow from the Boche! I recognise their handiwork. Ah! The scoundrels! The scoundrels!"

Then, kneeling on the edge of the tomb in order to examine more closely the victim of this most odious of crimes, this vilest betrayal, Chantecoq, raising his hat, reached towards the cadaver while saying, shaking with energy and indignation, "Colonel, you will be avenged, I swear!

"And now that I've recovered the victim, I must uncover the murderer!"

***

Chantecoq quickly got a grip on himself.

"This isn't the time to shoot myself in the foot," he murmured. "It's broad daylight, and though this chapel is barely frequented by the faithful, let alone miscreants, a curious soul might wander in all the same. It would be truly daft to be discovered with the body of this poor Colonel."

Standing again, the policeman calmly, as if he was accomplishing the simplest task in the world, replaced the slab that he'd lifted, removing, with a subtlety that the unfortunate Colonel's murderers had lacked, all trace of the breaking and entering he had just committed.

Leaving the old, ruined sanctuary, the detective returned outside.

For a good two minutes, he remained watchful, his ears straining.

Then he murmured, "All clear! That's some good work, in fact... Come now, I'm not too displeased with myself today."

But, while stifling an involuntary yawn, Chantecoq added, "Hold on! Hold on, hold on! Could it be that I'm tired, by any chance? My word, you could say so... heavy brain and rubbery legs... it's a bad sign, my boy!

"But after all, it's hardly extraordinary. Since I arrived in Douai, I'm sure I've not slept a full quarter of a night. We might be built from reinforced concrete, but that's hardly sufficient for a man who needs all his imagination and strength.

"That's why, old Chantecoq, I'm ordering you, before you get back to work, take a complete rest, absolute, for two hours. After that, you'll be back on form, and you can 'work' as you need to."

Spotting a copse of young trees bordering a neighbouring field, whose leaves formed a sufficient obstacle to the rays of the sun which, as evening approached, were beginning to wane, the bloodhound made his way over without haste, and lay down.

"It's quarter to five. Let's set the alarm for seven. That will be a good rest. Now, good evening world, and let's pause our little tale."

A few seconds later, Chantecoq was snoring.

At precisely seven o'clock, as though a buzzer had rung next to him, the policeman, with one abrupt movement, rose from his bed, fresh, alert, a smile on his lips.

This truly extraordinary man indeed possessed not only the precious faculty of falling asleep at will, and waking in the same way, but he also passed, without the slightest hesitation, from a state of sleeping to full wakefulness, recovering instantly, as soon as he raised his eyelids, all his faculties, all his vigour, and all his presence of mind.

"That's better!" he said, breathing deeply, "but, I must confess I'm hungry. My word, yes, I even feel I've quite a hearty appetite! Shall we break a crust?"

Chantecoq reached into a pocket which was hidden in his tunic's lining, and took out a small flask with the capacity of around quarter of a litre. It contained a reddish liquid, of which he drank a few mouthfuls.

After recorking the bottle carefully, he replaced it in his pocket, saying, "Now that I've dined, we'll allow ourselves the luxury of smoking a fine pipe."

This time, it was from his trouser pocket that the bloodhound took out a large briar root pipe which he stuffed methodically with *Caporal Ordinaire* tobacco. He lit it, took several voluptuously deep lungfuls; then, lying on his back, he said while giving a deep sigh of satisfaction:

"Now, let's think long, and think hard."

At first, the policeman's gaze remained as though enveloped by a vague, opaque fog. Then, little by little, it regained a certain animation, and soon shone with ever-increasing light… while monosyllables, clipped words, in no particular order, escaped his lips as though in spite of him.

"The Lieutenant perhaps? Yet he doesn't give the impression… He would have managed to fool everyone around him… No, I can't believe such a thing! In the end, though, all the same… I suspected it wouldn't be convenient… but, my word, I'd never have believed…"

Noticing he had let his pipe go out, he cried as though he was speaking to a human being, "Oh! My poor Joséphine! My old friend, my faithful confidante, have I let you

61

extinguish yourself? Ah yes, dash it! Eh! You must be used to it? But never mind, I offer my most sincere apologies."

Relighting his pipe, Chantecoq went back to the horizontal position which he had abandoned for a moment, and returned to his thoughts.

Night was falling.

Across the dusk, between the lacy leaves of the oaks, the bloodhound noticed some corners of the sky populated by stars.

The sunset was superb.

Chantecoq's face, whose features contracted towards one thought, had displayed if not hardness then a tenacious, indomitable will, relaxed into an expression of infinite generosity.

Two words, two simple words of affected pity, escaped his lips. "Poor mite!"

It was in the middle of these ardent, contradictory, anguished, tragic reflections, that the adorable silhouette of the pretty Yvonne had just appeared.

"Yes, poor mite!" he repeated with a tender tone which hardly seemed usual for him.

"How great her sorrow will be! She loved her father so much! How much is she going to suffer when she learns he was treacherously assassinated by… by whom?"

And jumping up, the policeman murmured in a heavy, anguished voice. "My God, as long as it wasn't Lieutenant Vallier who, having betrayed his boss and fallen under suspicion, lured the Colonel into a trap in order to be rid of him…

"And yet, I've observed this young man closely. Nothing in his attitude appeared louche to me… I've rummaged around in his past, he is irreproachable.

"And would he have played out this shameful little drama for love? Why? With what purpose?"

"No, it's not possible. This distinguished officer who, it appears, is an admirable son, who seems to love that young girl in a fashion as ardent as ~~disinterested~~, was ready to sacrifice himself, to exile himself, so as not to trouble her calm. *it is selfless*

"Yes, but perhaps that's all the skilful manoeuvring of a wretch who, having long premeditated his crime, begins, before executing it, by taking every precaution to evade justice…

"This boy with such sympathetic features, a mind so loyal, so sincere, would be nothing less than the most abominable of scoundrels. That would truly be too horrible! This child, already struck so cruelly by the loss of her paternal love… how torn, devastated, would she be if she learned the murderer of her father was none other than the man she loved!

"She is so charming, so gentle… She seems so good and pure. When she looks at you, you'd say it's as though the heavens move through you…

"Certainly, I no longer believe in much. I've seen so much, of all sorts, and of all shades… But that's all the same… Mademoiselle Yvonne, she must be enough to make you believe in the Good Lord, because only the Good Lord could create such angels!"

Repressing the intense emotion which, without him knowing and much in spite of his will, had burst from him, Chantecoq cried in a nervous, agitated tone: "That's enough! See now how, instead of acting, I indulge in sentiment like a midinette![3]

[3] A fashionable but vacuous young lady. The modern equivalent might be "bimbo".

63

"And what's more, I've again left my old friend to extinguish herself. This is stupid!"

While relighting his pipe for the third time, Chantecoq continued, pursuing his dialogue with her whom he called his confidant.

"My poor Joséphine, you must be forming a very sad picture of your old comrade.

"No? Not too bad? How indulgent you are! Eh! What's that you say to all this? Vicious business, wasn't it? You believe I should see it through? ~~My~~ too, my goodness! Only, there we are! We must... yes, what must we do? Ah, yes, goodness, that's it...

"You've just given another good piece of advice. You're right, a hundred times right... always right... Let's see, let's see, let's put my ideas in some form of order!

"First to assure myself whether Lieutenant Vallier is guilty... or innocent. That's where we must begin, isn't it? Yes... perfect!

"How the devil do we establish that?

"Don't you have any more ideas, my dear Joséphine... you who have so many?"

As though he was really waiting for a response from his 'old friend', Chantecoq remained silent, while staring obstinately at the blueish smoke which escaped from the furnace of his pipe.

Observing it was rising in little puffy clouds towards the Chapelle Saint-Nicolas, he continued in a satisfied, tranquil tone. "There it is, that's it, that's really it! I understand, thank you my friend!"

Jumping to his feet in one movement, he shook the ash from his pipe while saying, "Go to sleep, dear Joséphine. Go!

Meanwhile, I believe your old comrade will not be short of work tonight."

Chantecoq, with a discreet, muffled, careful gait, headed back to the chapel.

He emerged again half an hour later, carrying under his arm a rather voluminous parcel, wrapped in its black envelope.

Then, using the back of his sleeve to wipe away the sweat which beaded his forehead, the policeman murmured, "A nasty job, but necessary. Now, my little lad, as they say in theatre, on stage for Act One!"

9 THE REVENANT

A patrol circulating between midnight and one o'clock in the morning around the Douai powder mill would not have failed to collide with an officer who, the collar of his uniform coat raised up to his ears, and his kepi jammed down over his eyes, was prowling the boundary wall which defended the military factory against incursion.

But the surroundings were deserted. And if, from time to time, heavy echoing footsteps could be heard from the sentry who stood before the entrance gate, no bayonet gleamed in the night. All was calm, silent. Everything was at rest.

The officer, an engineer Colonel, soon paused, consulted his watch, and murmured, "They've done their rounds, now I'm calm. I've two hours before me, more than I need to do my work."

Then Chantecoq (for it was he), who, with marvellous, incomparable art had succeeded in bringing back to life an extraordinarily realistic Colonel Richard, striking in resemblance, approached a small door lodged in the wall, drew a keychain from his pocket, chose one, jiggled the lock… and entered the interior courtyard like a shadow, a true ghost.

Without the slightest hurry, he reached the red brick house, entered the hallway and, lighting a pocket flashlight, he took a new key from his chain, calmly opened the door which led to the Colonel's office, and slipped inside.

"Now," he said to himself, "the hardest part is done…"

Approaching the window, he rattled the hasp, reached his arm outside, pushed a shutter closed.

Then, returning to the Colonel's workbench, he turned the switch.

The room lit up in a discreet fashion.

The detective looked around. He looked for a corner to put himself, away from the light, in the shadows, as though he wanted, if not to hide entirely, at least to avoid close scrutiny.

Soon he decided. He knelt before a filing cabinet, from which he took some files that, without even taking the trouble to leaf through them, he scattered on the floor, when suddenly his gaze fell on a letter that looked as though it had been crumpled, ready to be discarded, and ~~that had~~ been *which had then* picked up again in order to keep it… with care.

The policeman read it with care too.

"Oh! Oh!" he said, "this is something out of the ordinary, and might help us." Calmly he folded the note and tucked it into the pocket of his coat.

Then he waited.

A slight tremor in his hands revealed he was prey to a certain anxiety, which was soon expressed with these words: "As long as he comes! And yet, I'm sure he'll have to spend the night in his office, to finish the report his bosses ordered on the artillery park explosion. To think it might have been him who…"

But the policeman stopped.

It seemed to him that a footstep could be heard at the end of the corridor.

"There he is!" murmured Chantecoq, or rather the Colonel's shade.

The footsteps approached.

The door opened.

Raymond Vallier appeared.

The bloodhound, who pretended to have seen and heard nothing, seemed more and more engrossed in his research into important files.

The Lieutenant, whose face already bore the traces of profound surprise, remained rooted to the spot.

A cry escaped his throat: "Colonel!"

The fake Richard then raised his head.

With an authoritative gesture, he tried to impose silence on the young officer.

But this man darted towards him whom he took for his boss, crying with a tone of indescribable joy, ringing with the most generous sincerity,

"Ah! Colonel! Colonel, you've returned! How happy I am and how happy your daughter will be!"

Chantecoq was relieved.

He was at peace.

The experiment had succeeded.

Not only had Lieutenant Vallier mistaken him for Colonel Richard, but from that cry torn so spontaneously from his heart, the bloodhound now had the right and the duty to say to himself, "this man is innocent!"

Deep joy erupted in him, at the same time as violent remorse for ~~having~~ suspect*ing*, even for an instant, this man, this French officer, whose loyalty now appeared to be immaculate, radiant.

What a weight off the mind of the ardent patriot that Chantecoq was! What a relief, what a deliverance to be able to say to himself: "It isn't one of our own who is the traitor."

Now that he was certain, what was he going to do?

Reveal his subterfuge, or continue playing his role?

Chantecoq seemed to hesitate.

He looked at the young man before him with an expression of intense but contained emotion.

He was ready to launch himself towards him, to swear everything to him, to beg his pardon for having used such a method to discover the truth.

But suddenly a flicker of triumphant intellect, even of divination, lit up in his eyes.

There was no doubt that an immense thought, the mother of a gigantic project, had just illuminated his brain.

So in a low voice, in the mysterious tone of confiding a secret, with the same intonations of he from whom he had taken not just the uniform, but the whole character, Chantecoq declared:

"Lieutenant Vallier, not one word, not one movement. Until further orders, it's essential that everyone, even Yvonne, believes me to have disappeared, and that no one knows where I am!"

The moment was truly tragic.

Still in shadow, the revenant seems to hypnotise the young officer with his superior will, while the young officer who, troubled beyond all expression, babbles, "Colonel, let me tell you… Mademoiselle Yvonne is so unhappy!"

search for '.' or '.,'.

But the detective answers, still in the same low voice, and now a little trembling.

"No. No, what you're asking of me is impossible. For some time yet, I must stay in the shadows. It's necessary, not just for my own honour, but for your happiness, for that of…"

Chantecoq stops, as though he ~~felt~~ *feels* too much remorse to speak any more of it.

But Lieutenant Vallier, breathless, asks. "That of…?"

The fake Monsieur Richard then drops the decisive word…

"That of…" he dares not say *my daughter!*

He says simply. "That of Yvonne."

"What! You would finally consent…?" exclaim*s* the young man.

So Chantecoq takes his hand and declares with an emotion he no longer seeks to hide.

"Know that I have just one remaining goal in life: that's to unite the two of you."

"Colonel!" exclaims the Lieutenant, who, in a movement of distraught gratitude, goes to throw himself into the arms of the man he takes to be his boss.

But the policeman, with a gesture full of authority, stops him while saying. "You'll swear to me to remain silent."

"As you demand, Colonel, so I swear to you," Vallier obeys instantly.

But then, suddenly, both men start with shock.

The noise of a slamming door has just been heard, from the side of the Richards' quarters.

Vallier, with an instinctive movement, heads towards the window and looks outside, while Chantecoq, immobile, waits.

"Mademoiselle Yvonne…" Raymond murmurs.

"Her!" the detective starts, paling beneath his make-up.

And he murmurs. "She mustn't see me!"

He tiptoes over to the window.

"Where is she?" he asks the Lieutenant in a low voice.

"She disappeared," says the young man. "She's bypassing the building to come here."

Chantecoq, with a decisive tone, simply orders, "Withdraw."

Vallier vanishes from the room.

The false-Colonel wedges open the window and jumps into the courtyard.

He has to get away… pressed against the walls, looking for shadows.

But suddenly a female voice calls out in the night, close by him.

It's Yvonne who, having heard the very slight sound the policeman made in crossing the window frame and falling to the ground, has retraced her steps and runs towards him.

"Who's there? Who are you?" the young girl asks bravely.

Chantecoq sharply looks to hide his face under the collar of his coat.

But he is too late.

Yvonne gives out a terrible cry.

Thanks to the moon's vague, but sufficient, light on the factory courtyard, she recognises the uniform, the shape, the pace of the Colonel.

"Father! My father!" Beating the air with her hands, she collapses with a cry composed of both stupor and joy.

The detective remains undecided for a moment.

It could be said that a painful stupor roots him to the spot.

71

But a man comes running.

It's Lieutenant Vallier.

In the shadows, he can make out Yvonne's body on the ground, inanimate, and close to him, standing, immobile, the man he believes to be her father.

"Colonel!" Raymond cries. "Have pity on her!"

"Silence, now more than ever!" the false Richard orders. "She didn't see me, you hear? She was dreaming… it wasn't me! I beg you, I order you, more than ever! Not a word, even to my own daughter. This is for the honour of my name, for the glory of France!"

And while dominated, subjugated, the artillery Lieutenant remains silent, Chantecoq disappears into the night.

10 EXPLOSIVE Z

It was a strange dwelling, that of Monsieur Jean Aubry, the famous inventor of the Combat Aircraft.

At first glance, however, it offered nothing unusual.

Situated in one of the quietest streets in Saint-Mandé, it consisted of a house surrounded by a carefully maintained flowering garden, defended by a light palisade of green slats painted green and garnished on the outside by a privet hedge.

In the middle, there was a rickety gate which functioned by means of a simple copper handle.

Above a wooden letterbox, an inscription or rather a word engraved on the top half of the gate: "Enter!"

Now, as soon as the visitor, so benevolently welcomed in advance, crossed the threshold and stepped into the garden, if his eye halted with a certain complacency over the surrounding objects, he would soon discover, behind the espaliers where fruit trees grew, and trellises along the length of which swarmed beautiful roses, some minuscule wires hooked up to the walls with white porcelain insulators and which, cleverly entangled, disappeared in every direction.

But things became complicated, in a way as strange as it was unexpected, when one entered the house.

Hardly had one planted a foot on the straw mat placed in the hallway, when suddenly, with lightning rapidity, two steel grilles, sliding the length of the partitions, sprang up, one before you, the other behind, holding you prisoner, while a powerful electric siren rang inside the house.

That particular day, his visitor - a Colonel - had just been caught in the cage.

While the officer, bursting out laughing, cried, "Ah! What a great demonstration!" a tall man, with a physiognomy that was intelligent and energetic, tumbled down the staircase and, facing the captive, who appeared greatly amused by the surprise he had received, spoke in a deep and resonant voice.

"If I'm not mistaken… it's Colonel Richard…"

Before this last had time to speak a word, the grilles slid back into the ground with the same speed with which they had surged from it.

Then, advancing, his hand held out, towards his guest, Jean Aubry cried out, "My sincere apologies, Colonel. But after the adventure that befell me…"

"Ah! Yes, the Combat Aircraft…"

"I'm obliged to take great precautions."

"You're right," nodded the officer who, with a tone of perfect good humour added, "all the same, it's hardly easy to enter your home."

"It's even more difficult to leave it."

"So I notice."

"Again, please accept my most sincere apologies, Colonel."

"But to the contrary, it's fine, totally fine."

"Would you, Colonel, do me the honour of coming up to my laboratory? We'll have peace and quiet there, and be completely at ease to talk."

"Gladly, dear Monsieur Aubry."

"May I show you the way?"

"If you would."

The inventor, followed by the officer, quickly climbed a staircase which ended in a fairly narrow landing.

There, Jean Aubry opened a door which had the peculiarity of being constructed entirely from aluminium; and stepping aside politely, he gestured inside. "Go in then, Colonel."

The Colonel stepped into a huge room which took up the entire first floor of the house.

It was a real chemist's laboratory, equipped not only with the usual furnaces, retorts and crucibles, but with still more of all sorts of devices, of the most varied and unusual shapes.

A vast wardrobe of the same metal as the door took up a whole panel.

Opposite, a library without windows aligned several rows of thick books. Each of their spine carried, in solid gold characters, a letter followed by a number.

Jean Aubry pointed out an old couch, piled high with files, where there was barely any room to sit.

He remained standing, leaning lightly on a trestle table on which an unfinished blueprint was pinned with gold-headed nails.

Then, in welcoming tones imprinted with the greatest deference, the inventor began. "To what do I owe, Colonel, the honour and pleasure of your visit?"

"Do you not suspect it, even a little?" the fake Richard responded in a tone of the frankest and most cordial bonhomie.

"Would it be on the subject of the explosive?"

"Precisely."

"There's something not working?"

"I confess I am extremely embarrassed."

"How so?"

"This is all between us, isn't it?"

"Naturally."

"First, I won't hide from you, my dear Monsieur Aubry, that I'm scared of the responsibility incumbent on me."

"Scared, what for?"

"You'll be the first to acknowledge your explosive's manufacture is the most delicate process."

"Certainly. But aren't you the most distinguished, most renowned pyro-technician in the army?"

"You're exaggerating!"

"And you, you're too modest."

"There are other reasons."

"What other reasons?"

"I fear the Douai powder mill may not be sufficiently equipped for the work we've entrusted to it."

"That astonishes me. The Minister of War declared the contrary to me. In any case, it's an inconvenience that's easily remedied."

"But that's not all," insisted the pseudo-officer.

"Speak, I beg you!"

"I will swear to you frankly that, in the formula the engineer of powders and saltpetre communicated to me... Oh! I beg you, don't freeze at what I'm about to tell you... there are certain details I didn't grasp."

"What's that?" Jean Aubry exclaimed with a violent start.

And immediately, his forehead gloomy, his voice curt, he added, "I don't understand. For a man with a career like yours, it ought to have been thoroughly clear."

"I'm telling you, to the contrary, that there are doubtful points which need to be illuminated, notably regarding a specific dose of nitro-glycerine."

"Nitro-glycerine!" the inventor interrupted violently. "But there's not a single molecule of it in the composition of my explosive."

"I assure you there is…"

"No. See here, this isn't possible."

"I repeat, Monsieur Aubry, that I'm not mistaken. I've read it, and I asked myself…"

"If I had gone mad?" the chemist interrupted. "I took, to the contrary, the greatest care to avoid that product, which has no reason to exist."

"That's just what I thought."

Then, more and more irritated, Aubry continued. "Damn! I see too clearly! It's yet another process from those gentlemen bureaucrats. They'll have wanted to add their grain of salt to my new invention, to prove their value in the eyes of their bosses!"

"Ah! I recognise that story all too well!"

Then, walking straight up to his associate, he asked brusquely. "Do you have the formula?"

The false officer, who had doubtless anticipated this very question, replied immediately, with the greatest sang-froid in the world.

"My dear Monsieur Aubry, I didn't believe it prudent to bring it with me. I thought it wiser to leave it in Douai, in a place where no one can discover it. We are infested with spies, and their audacity is extraordinary."

"I know the feeling, Colonel!"

Still in the same tone of cordial bonhomie, the fake Richard continued. "Believe me, I have in my head the formula communicated to me by the Minister. It's sufficient to compare it to your own."

"My own no longer, it's not here."

"What's that?" said the visitor with a slight reaction of disappointment.

"The Minister, not that he had concerns over my good faith - because, better than anyone, he knows that it's above all suspicion - but purely as a precaution, made me give my word of honour to destroy all documents relating to my new invention.

"While this measure was completely useless, sure as I am that my formula was much more secure here than anywhere else, I didn't want to discuss it. I obeyed!"

"That's deeply regrettable," the Colonel engineer stressed, while his lips pursed beneath his thick white moustache.

"We can sort everything out very easily," Jean Aubry reassured him, "we only have to head over to the Ministry straight away. I'll ask that they communicate to me immediately all the documents relating to Explosive Z, and we can set about the necessary checks."

This offer, despite being so simple and so natural, didn't appear to make the officer smile.

Because in a tone full of gentle conciliation, he replied, "Certainly, there's an excellent idea. However, dear sir, would you allow me not to subscribe immediately?"

"And why's that?"

"You just yourself told me that you strongly suspect the offices of making this adjustment!"

"Exactly, this is an admirable opportunity to unmask them."

"An admirable opportunity for you, I'm sure! But, as you want to do me a great favour, allow me to beg you, in these very delicate circumstances, to think a little of me. If there's a scandal, you will come out of it triumphant.

"But I, who will have been the one who provoked it, what vengeance, what reprisals will I receive from an opposition much too strong for anyone to dream of reducing it or beating it.

"I still have a few years of service ahead of me. I hope to become a General. I have a daughter, I have no fortune…"

"Say no more, Colonel, I understand. I won't insist. I'll sort everything out in any case, without compromising you."

"I am infinitely beholden to you."

"All this is between us, isn't it?"

"Of course, Monsieur Aubry!"

"Your word of honour?"

"My word of honour."

"I'll reconstitute my formula, and will communicate it to you."

"Thank you, with all my heart," said the impostor, holding both hands to the inventor, who grasped them and shook them with effusion, while crying out:

"I'm all too happy to be of service and at the same time to frustrate this criminal intrigues."

Jean Aubry headed towards a small desk at which he sat down.

Taking a sheet of paper from a binder, he began to write down numbers, letters, in a clean, consistent hand.

Then standing up and returning, paper in hand, towards his visitor who, impassive in appearance, and remaining at a discreet distance, was making a huge effort to hide the intense joy that had taken hold of him, he said, "There we are, you see it's not all that difficult…"

With a hand that trembled slightly, Colonel Richard's lookalike was about to seize the precious document when, brusquely, Jean Aubry cried out.

"In fact, now I think of it! Didn't you tell me, Colonel, that you lack in Douai the material necessary for the manufacture of Explosive Z?"

"That's right," the engineering officer had to acknowledge, somewhat taken aback.

Then, folding his paper in four and placing it in a wallet that he had taken in the interior pocket of his redingote, Aubry declared:

"Do you know what we're going to do? Ah well! We'll set off together this evening for Douai; and there, after comparing our two formulae and checking the machines, we'll see. Having remedied the machines' imperfections, which is in the realm of the possible, we'll recommence manufacture, as I conceived it, and without anyone suspecting a thing. Does that suit you?"

"Absolutely," agreed the visitor, who seemed to have regained all his aplomb and sang-froid.

"Then it's agreed!" the chemist concluded. "What time does your train leave?"

"At eight twenty-five."

"We'll meet at eight, at Gare du Nord."

"Dear Monsieur Aubry," gushed the fake Richard, now smiling again. "Would you do me one more great honour?"

"Gladly, Colonel!"

"Be on the terrace of the cafe Terminus at seven o'clock, we'll dine together."

"I accept!"

"Until then!"

"I can add only one thing, my dear Colonel. I congratulate myself that the government entrusted the job of manufacturing my explosive to a man as intelligent and conscientious as you."

"You flatter me!"

"So, until this evening?"

"Seven o'clock at Terminus?"

"Seven, at Terminus."

Monsieur Aubry led the Colonel back to the garden door.

On the threshold, both men again shook hands.

While Jean Aubry retreated back inside, the pseudo-Director of the Douai powder mill headed to the tramway from Vincennes to Paris.

But, shortly before arriving at the station, he turned off into a deserted street where a car was parked, with a chassis that was both soberly elegant and hermetically sealed.

On the seat, a driver in impeccable livery was sitting stiffly, immobile, awaiting orders.

As the Colonel approached the car, a door opened, revealing a woman's hand in a fine black glove, while an impatient voice called, "So?"

"It's going to work," replied the pseudo-Richard, sitting down next to a woman dressed in sombre clothes whose face was covered by an impenetrable veil.

The limousine pulled away.

The veiled lady spoke. "So, Colonel von Reitzer, you succeeded?"

"I have him, dear Madame… Férel," the German officer replied simply.

"Finally!" Wilhelm's spy cried in a voice trembling with joy.

11 A STUMBLING BLOCK

Jean Aubry, after having been for lunch in a local restaurant as was his habit, returned home, to pick up his work.

He was not exactly in a good mood.

Indeed, he was reflecting on the morning's incident.

Far from suspecting the true identity of the wretch who, with stupefying audacity and infernal cunning, had succeeded in tricking his way into his home and entirely abusing his good faith, the famous inventor, convinced he had dealt with Colonel Richard in the flesh, was grumbling.

"Bureaucrats again! Always bureaucrats! What a mindset! What a mentality!

"The new Minister of War, Monsieur Mazurier, is a man with a firm grasp on things, and I'm sure he'd be only too happy to take my part. Only I wouldn't want to compromise the brave Colonel.

"However, once I've sorted everything out, I'll see if there's a way to resolve this state of affairs which is so prejudicial to the interests of National Defence."

As he gave this private monologue, Jean Aubry reached his home.

Taking a small key that he always carried in his fob, he quickly opened the letterbox which was fixed to one of the gates.

It contained nothing more than a telegram.

The genius took it, closed the box, then, while entering his garden, tore along the dotted line of the little note which he began to read with a distracted, indifferent air.

But soon his attitude was transformed.

His face took on an expression of preoccupied surprise.

An exclamation pronounced in the gravest tones escaped him. "Devil!"

With a brusque gesture, Jean Aubry was about to banish the mysterious missive to his pocket when, changing his mind, he felt it necessary to reread a second time.

It was composed thus:

My dear friend,
Come to meet me, drop everything.
I've extremely important news for you.
It's enough for you to know that there's another plot by those filthy B***, and we must frustrate it as quickly as possible.
I'm counting on you to get here with the briefest delay, because there is great urgency and, more than any other, you're involved in this very serious tale.
I await you, at home, and I shan't leave before seeing you.
But, please, be diligent. There is not a minute to lose.
I'm counting on you. Apologies and kind regards. Your devoted,
CHANTECOQ

"Ah! What can be going on?" the inventor wondered, anxious. "Has some accident befallen my son-in-law, Captain Evrard? No, just this morning I received a letter from my daughter, telling me they're both enjoying themselves greatly at Maubeuge and that they're in excellent health.

"However, misfortune strikes so swiftly. The Germans haven't forgiven my dear and valiant Germaine, or my son-in-law, or myself, for the tricks we played on them in Germany. They wrap all three of us up in the same hatred, as well as brave Chantecoq, their *bête noire*, deservedly.

"But as my friend recommends, let's not waste any time, and set off for Paris!"

Returning outside, Monsieur Aubry headed towards the nearest tramway station, went down to the gates, and was engulfed by the Metro.

Around two in the afternoon, he rang the bell of a small apartment situated on the fifth floor of a comfortable building on Avenue Trudaine.

Crisp footsteps rang out immediately in the hallway.

The door swung open.

Chantecoq's silhouette appeared, illuminated, it seemed to the great inventor, by beams of the most acute satisfaction.

"You, my dear friend," he exclaimed. "Just in time! But come in, I beg you."

The detective showed the inventor into a cramped office, very simply furnished, then, waving him towards an armchair, he said cordially, "Sit down and make yourself at home. We have to speak at length, and seriously."

"Just one question?" the inventor asked.

"Please, go on."

"I hope you don't have any bad news for me concerning the children?"

Aubry spoke the word 'children' with a tender inflection which contrasted somewhat with the severe and even slightly rude aspect of his character.

The bloodhound rushed to reassure him. "Don't worry. This has nothing to do with our dear Germaine, who as you know, I love with all my heart. It's also unconnected to Captain Evrard whom I consider one of the French army's most brilliant officers. On returning home this morning, I even found two lovely cards from them."

"Me too," the father said, completely reassured. "Today I received some very good news. But… one never knows… all sorts of ideas came into my head."

"There you are then, no need to worry about them," exclaimed Chantecoq, while clasping the genius's hands affectionately.

While that brave man was sitting down, the detective continued. "My poor friend, I caused you real anxiety, without meaning to. I ought to have been more precise. But I swear it never occurred to me. At the moment I have so many things in my head, and I've just been mixed up in events which were *so* extraordinary, I could go so far as to say *so* tragic, it pushed me into displaying a negligence that I hope you will forgive."

"It's I who was ridiculous to torment myself," Jean Aubry affirmed. "Let's think no more of it, because now I'm anxious to be brought up to date with these events…"

Chantecoq cut him off. "It's unimaginable! It goes without saying, doesn't it, to ask you that until further notice this is all to be treated with the utmost secrecy?"

"You have my word!"

"Very well, here goes!" the policeman began. "Several days ago, the Minister of War summoned me to his office

86

and, at the suggestion of the director of Sûreté générale, he assigned me the mission of leading an enquiry at the Douai powder mill, where they had reason to believe a German spy had infiltrated.

"Following a first meeting with the director, Colonel Richard, a very brave man, incidentally…" to add

"Absolutely," Aubry felt he ~~had to~~ ought ʌ as a true savant. —

Chantecoq pressed on. "I became certain the Minister wasn't mistaken. I'll even tell you that my suspicions at first fell on a young Lieutenant named Raymond Vallier, to the point of testing him, but I hasten to add that, happily, I since acquired clear proof that my doubts were unfounded.

"In brief, the Colonel and I agreed I should carry out over the powder mill a surveillance that was as discreet as it was active. We even arranged that I would come to his office the following day in the guise of an engineer, and that I would immediately begin my investigations… when a huge explosion interrupted our conversation. It was the artillery park exploding!"

"Indeed, I read about that, in the papers…"

"You'll see, it's not finished," replied Chantecoq, who was getting warmed up in his tale. "Ceding to an entirely natural curious impulse, I rushed outside, leaving my Colonel there and running towards the sinister site… where I could only observe the results of the catastrophe, and gather information which confirmed my opinion that the accident had nothing to do with negligence or misfortune, but was the work of that criminal hand which infiltrates everywhere around us, with the aim of abominable destruction."

The inventor of Explosive Z ground his teeth. "I know those all too well, the wretches!"

87

"But all this is nothing yet," declared the detective. "After spending several hours at the scene of the crime, I returned to the hotel to organise the notes I'd taken, and to compose a long encrypted telegram to the minister. Then, the following morning, after transforming myself into the guise of an engineer, I passed via the post office to send my dispatch and reached the powder mill, where I had a meeting with Colonel Richard.

"How can I express, my dear friend, my stupefaction on finding his daughter in tears! Her father had vanished. I'm skipping over a few details that I'll tell you soon, if you judge it useful.

"I now arrive at the terrible, capital detail, which will prove to you that once again we find ourselves facing a conspiracy, hatched against us by the great German spy network.

"The same day, I discovered that Colonel Richard had been assassinated."

At those words, Monsieur Aubry, who had listened to his friend with the calmest and most sustained attention, raised his head sharply.

"Colonel... Richard... assassinated..." he repeated. In the deepest shock.

"Just so... ass-ass-in-at-ed," stressed Chantecoq, emphasising each syllable.

The great scholar replied. "I believe, my dear friend, that this time, quite against your usual habits, and may it be said without offending you, you are absolutely on the wrong tack."

The detective, not put out in the least, asked him with a gently ironic air, "On what basis do you offer such a hypothesis?"

"It's very simple," responded the inventor of the combat aircraft, who had never seemed more sure of himself. In a firm voice which revealed no trace of emotion, he explained. "Barely three hours ago, Colonel Richard was at Saint-Mandé."

"What are you saying?" the policeman literally jumped.

"I'm saying, dear friend, that Colonel Richard found himself this morning, between eleven and noon, at my home, in my laboratory."

"That's impossible!" Chantecoq snapped back, in the grip of strong emotion.

"I assure you, my friend," Germaine's father insisted, "I spoke to him at great length and…"

The detective cut him off sharply with a tone of absolute authority. "And I swear to you that I saw him lying dead, frozen, covered in blood, in a vault where his murderers hid him. I'll add that I myself divested him of his clothes, which I needed, and as I closed his eyes with my own hands, I begged his pardon for this act of sacrilege that I judged to be vital for truth to triumph."

"But, then, this man I saw at my home this morning?" Aubry asked, scared.

"It was yet another spy!" roared Chantecoq, whose eyes were blazing.

"Indeed! I can tell you something…" said the inventor, shaken by a powerful chill. "I was lucky to escape him!"

"My word!" replied Chantecoq, "I didn't believe they would go so far. But that's not all! More than ever we'll need all our resolve, all our calm. Just one word more, dear friend…"

"What?"

"You handed over none of your secrets to this bandit, right?"

"Nothing… but it was close, I swear it."

"You're also sure he couldn't have stolen anything from you?"

"I'm sure of it."

"I can breathe again… and now it's your turn to tell me how all this happened."

Jean Aubry, with perfect precision, gave his associate a complete and detailed account of his interview with the fake Colonel Richard.

When he had finished, Chantecoq, who hadn't interrupted him once, cried out, "Goodness! It's clear as mud. OK with Richard… the real one… I took the precaution of destroying his formula for your Explosive Z, such was my feeling that there was in position one of those rogues who would stop at nothing to achieve their goal.

"Now events are piecing themselves together… After his crime, not having found the document he coveted, this brigand must have taken the path of seeking it from you. He had the same idea as me, he's taken on Richard's appearance. And was it well done?"

"Admirably, as I was taken in at once," acknowledged Jean Aubry, before adding, "I know I had seen the unfortunate officer only two or three times, and those quite rapidly."

The bloodhound shook his head. "That means nothing. This is a cheeky bunny we're dealing with. I thought I was the only one who could manage to pull off tricks of that kind. I've been disillusioned! What an injury to my self-respect!

"Ah! I can't deny, everything was admirably prepared, thought through, executed. If I wasn't sure Emma Lückner was safe in her final rest six feet beneath the ground, I could believe it was her who had orchestrated everything. But her, or another, what does it matter! You'll be thwarted, Boche gentlemen! It's your turn!

"Because, from this moment on, Chantecoq is preparing for you one of those stumbling blocks on which you'll break your nose. My dear Aubry, resume your place in that armchair whose arms you're holding, and listen to me carefully. We have work to do!"

12 A STRANGE DOCUMENT

The detective continued. "You have a meeting with our man this evening, at seven o'clock?"

"At Terminus, at Gare du Nord."

"Then everything's going well."

Monsieur

"Let me guess," declared Mr Aubry. "You're going to go and have him arrested."

"Hardly! I'll avoid that at all costs."

"Really!"

"My dear friend, you ought to know by now what these people are like. To bring down this spy, nothing, indeed, would be easier for me. But that would end only in a partial result. Once arrested, our Teutonic friend would shut himself away in the deepest muteness. Even supposing we manage to establish his true identity, which might not be as easy as you think, what good would it do us? One fewer, and that's it!"

"That's still something."

"Yes, but it's not enough! Indeed, that precipitous arrest would put the whole network in a state of high alert. They would go silent until a date impossible to predict. The enormous body blow that I'm planning, while tracking the coconut skilfully, saving me from inspiring the slightest suspicion in him, he will lead me fatally, and entirely without him knowing, into the viper's nest, which seems to be to me a remarkable specimen."

"Very true…" the inventor said approvingly, who straight away trusted his friend's instincts, so much did he profess for his policeman's genius a boundless admiration and limitless trust.

Chantecoq nodded. "Now I have them, and I'll make them my prey. Only we're going to have to maneuver. More than ever I feel I'm dealing with a strong opponent. And that's just how I like it.

"Much as the poet says: '*to vanquish without peril, is a triumph without glory*'[4] The struggle is going to be bloody, but… but… do you hear me, my dear Aubry, I shall have them here at home, just as I already had them on their own soil.

"In any case, now is not the time for speeches. Let's speak briefly, but let's speak well! What are you doing this afternoon?"

"I'm completely at your disposal."

Chantecoq's resolved tone revealed that his agile mind, so fertile in resources, had alighted on one of those plans which were a knack of his, and which were just as marvellous as they were unexpected. "So be it… so be it! My dear friend, can you wait here?"

"Gladly."

The detective continued. "I have an important task before me. I hope it won't require too much of my time. In any

[4] The poet in question is Pierre Corneille (1606-1684), and the line comes from *Le Cid* (1636) - "*A vaincre sans péril, on triomphe sans gloire*". Specialising in tragedies, Corneille was regarded as one of the three greatest seventeenth century French playwrights, along with Racine and Molière. Cardinal Richelieu (yes, that one) was his patron for some time, until a dispute over *Le Cid* breaching the unities.

case, you'll be good enough to wait for me patiently, and as soon as I return, we'll resume our conversation from where we left it. I beg your pardon for treating you like this."

And with an enigmatic smile, Chantecoq added: "Without doubt I'll need to do the same again."

"I'm always entirely at your disposal."

"It's just the task I have…"

"Good luck and I'll see you later."

"I'm not leaving yet. I need to go to my changing room first."

"Some further transformation?"

"Naturally, and it won't be the last one."

"I never dreamed it would be."

Then, pointing towards a table on which lay some papers and brochures, the detective added, "You may want to entertain yourself a little… will you excuse me?"

"Of course."

Chantecoq had already vanished.

Monsieur Aubry chose a broadsheet at random, but had hardly glanced at it when he let it fall next to him. A flood of sad, unsettling thoughts assailed him.

Shaken, completely overwhelmed by Chantecoq's revelation, he thought, "So we'll never be finished with that accursed race which infiltrates everywhere, which, tirelessly pursues its nefarious and devastating work from the shadows, abusing our overly chivalrous generosity, cynically violating the most sacred laws of hospitality, taking advantage of blindness, spinelessness, the negligence of those who ought to always keep one eye open, and knowing how to create the most accidental and as a consequence the most dangerous complicities, even in places which ought to be hermetically sealed against suspect gazes and indiscreet ears.

"What a diabolical method these Germans have for preparing for war! They make espionage into a true national institution.

"Subverted by cash reserves which refill as soon as they're emptied, they get in everywhere, stopping at nothing to acquire information, invading our homes, affecting polite manners, disinterested expressions, affirming to us with all the seriousness in the world that they love us dearly, that they find us to be very kind, very intelligent, very funny, that they wouldn't dream of attacking us, that instead they ask only to live alongside us with good intelligence, on the condition that we don't put too many shackles on their financial and commercial transactions, that we allow their industries all possible development, in a word that we grant breathing space to a people whose birth rate increases endlessly, imperiously demanding all manner of pacifist extensions that no one, according to them, could possibly refuse them…

"They tell you all this with smiles full of disingenuous bonhomie. They make themselves seem small, modest, even humble, going in their insistent steps, as far as platitude and baseness.

"And all the time, competing disastrously with our industry and our national commerce, they flood our market with their products of all kinds, while the Kaiser, hypocritically, addresses his most gracious smiles to us, their parliament votes for military credits on top of military credits, while the Krupp factories, civilisation's true hell, manufacture fearful engines in the shadows, their endlessly-reinforced army prepares for massacre, for fire, and for pillage, and their spies, rooted in our soil, the diabolical vanguard of the imperial hordes, try to weaken us, to disorient us, to murder us, before the time for battle has come.

"Ah! France... a country so noble and so loyal that you can't even open your eyes to the perfidy of the enemy who threatens you! When will you wake from your dream? When will you notice the danger within which threatens you? When, with a start of righteous anger, will you decide to crush under your heel the shameful battalion of spies that Wilhelm II is sending you?"

Jean Aubrey was so deep in his reflections, when the door was quietly opened.

A violent exclamation escaped his lips. "Oh really! This is too much!"

Colonel Richard, no longer in his Colonel's uniform, but in the most proper civilian clothes, stood before him.

Faced with this unexpected apparition, the inventor was stunned.

But the detective was approaching him, and in his most natural voice he began, "Come my dear friend, get over your shock. Because I must warn you, I'm preparing plenty more for you."

"Chantecoq..." murmured the scholar, still barely recovered from his surprise.

"By Jove," joked the bloodhound who seemed on great form, and in high spirits. "You ought to be used to my antics by now."

"That's true, because, with you, one must always be ready for anything."

"And for much more than that, eh?" And taking a sadder tone, Chantecoq added, "Poor Colonel Richard! His corpse has been toyed with quite enough! Only, with me, it's for the right cause. While they... ah! The scoundrels!

"Don't think I find it amusing to step into a dead man's shoes like this. If I hadn't been forced to do so by circumstances, I guarantee I would have been happy to avoid such a reincarnation.

"But what can you do? When one is saddled with such a task, without much choice as to methods, one takes the path that offers the greatest chance of success. And here it is!"

Jean Aubry replied, "Don't think that I disapprove; I'm completely of your opinion. Faced with such a vile adversary, one has the right, what am I saying, the duty to go to any and all lengths to unmask them and prevent them from inflicting harm. Only, I confess to you in all honesty that I don't really understand…"

"What? What don't you grasp?"

"Why disguise yourself as Colonel Richard in order to track down an individual who, in fact, has had the idea to impersonate the same man?"

"I foresaw this objection," acknowledged Chantecoq, "and I prepared a response. At the moment, it's not a question of trailing anybody. I'm going on an extremely important mission for which I'm forced, for the last time I hope, to play the role of our unfortunate Colonel.

"Anyway, I can certainly tell you its nature. But on condition, as always, that this new confidence will remain completely between us, until such time as I authorise you to make use of it."

"Yes, you secretive chap!" said Jean Aubry with a smile, used to the mysterious ways of his friend, who staked his pride as much as his policeman's caution on revealing his secrets only when he had achieved his goal, and won victory brilliantly.

Besides the inventor, of whom he was as sure as of himself, no one had ever been able to winkle the slightest confidence from him.

But, especially now Jean Aubry was tightly bound to this case, he doubtless acknowledged that it was vital to make him aware of some of his mysterious undertakings, because he replied, "Imagine that I found the strangest document among the poor Colonel's papers, which seemed to me bound to shed a little light on the mysterious events which have unfolded at the Douai powder mill over the last few days."

Taking from his pocket a sheet of paper folded in four, he passed it to Jean Aubry, saying, "Judge for yourself."

The scholar read quietly:

Paris 29 May 19..

Colonel

I know from the most reliable source that you are under threat at this moment both in terms of your own honour and your daughter's happiness.

I have some very serious revelations to make to you on this subject.

Unfortunately I am ill, very ill, and it's absolutely impossible for me to leave my sickbed.

In any case, the things I have to tell you are much too serious for me to be able to entrust them to paper. And would I have the strength necessary to reach the end of my task?

I would be very grateful if you could, between two trains, come to see me.

I swear to you that this is very serious and that you won't regret trusting a stranger who, in writing these lines to you, is aware of doing her duty as an honest Frenchwoman.

Oh! Yes… come… quickly, very quickly, because I greatly fear I don't have long to live.

Yours sincerely
Madeleine VERNIER
27, Rue Nollet
Paris

"How curious, indeed," observed the inventor, repeating some of the letter's first words. "You are under threat at this moment both in terms of your honour and your daughter's happiness."

At once, Jean Aubry asked, "So, you're going to visit this woman in that guise?"

"Naturally," said Chantecoq.

"Don't you worry that it might be a trap?"

"That's the first thing I thought. So, first thing this morning, I sought out some intelligence."

"And what did you learn?"

"That this Madeleine Vernier is the most honourable young lady, that she lives, with her blind old grandmother, on the proceeds of occasional piano lessons that she gives in the neighbourhood… as one fine day, exhausted from privations and hard work, she fell sick with consumption, and was given a short time to live."

"The poor woman!" said the excellent man that was Monsieur Aubry in all sincerity.

"So there's no time to lose," declared the detective. "Wait for me, because, on my return, I'll need your help."

"I'm completely at your disposal!"

"I'm counting on returning rather quickly."

"Take all the time you need."

"Until later!"

"Until later."

Chantecoq reached the door, when the inventor called him back.

"Tell me, my dear friend…"

"How can I be of service?"

"I just had a thought…"

"Tell me, please."

"Do you think there's any chance, as happens sometimes, that you'll find yourself face to face with the other Colonel Richard?"

"I've foreseen that tiresome possibility," responded the bloodhound. "And so… go over to the window and take a look."

Jean Aubry obeyed.

"What do you see down there, alongside the pavement?"

"A covered automobile."

"It's waiting for me, to take me from Avenue Trudaine to Rue Nollet, and from Rue Nollet back to Avenue Trudaine."

And with a frank peal of laughter, France's foremost copper added, "You see how simple it is; you just have to think ahead."

"However," objected the scholar, "you were unaware before my arrival that another Colonel Richard was wandering the capital's streets."

"Yes, but," the bloodhound was enjoying himself, "thanks to the little magic that a good fairy gifted to me, as soon as you warned me… I wished for this coach."

And, lowering his voice, in a comically confidential tone, he added, "Also, but don't tell anyone, I have a telephone in my bathroom."

Pivoting on his heels, Chantecoq reached the door, while the explosive's inventor was murmuring, "For sure, this man is a genius!"

13 REVELATIONS

"Grandmother, do you think he'll come?" a young woman sat in a rickety armchair asked with genuine anxiety. Despite the heat, she was wrapped up shivering in a woollen shawl.

"Yes, my darling," replied an elderly woman with white hair who, stooped and broken by age, instinctively directed her unseeing eyes towards her granddaughter, whose emaciated, feverish face, pale and cracked lips, and sunken chest shaken by a hoarse and almost incessant little cough, attested the incurable, fatal disease with which she was afflicted.

"I'm afraid, you see," said Madeleine Vernier. "I fear he didn't attach any importance to my letter."

"Why?"

"It's been more than eight days since I wrote to him, and no reply. Perhaps I expressed myself badly and wasn't convincing or persuasive enough? I've half a mind to send him a fresh letter."

"You'll tire yourself out again, my poor sweetheart."

"Who cares! Above all, I must not let such a misfortune happen! That young lady, although I don't know her, though I've never seen her... she's so kind to me! I know she's pretty and kind... And her father... a French officer... something frightful... irreparable! It seems to me I would do better if I was relieved of this weight which crushes me, which stifles me, which is killing me."

A tearing coughing fit interrupted the poor girl again, she brought a handkerchief to her lips, on which some reddish stains soon appeared.

Her grandmother understood without seeing them.

While tears sprang to the corners of her withered eyelids, she approached her child, cradling her in her arms, caressing her... calling her the most tender names.

It was all the blind woman could do for the sickly creature who was snuggled against her, a little calmed, a little reinvigorated by the warmth of this touching and maternal affection.

Then Madame Vernier said, "Would you like me to call our neighbour? You know how compassionate and devoted she is. She'd like nothing better than to prepare a warm infusion which will do you good."

"I wouldn't want to disturb her again."

"She's only asking to help us..."

"I know."

"Let me do it. I only have to knock on the partition wall, as usual, She'd come at once."

"No, grandmother."

"Yes, my darling, I will rest easier. Oh! What misfortune that I no longer see clearly, and that I can't care for you as I'd like..."

"Oh! You're so good, nothing but your presence gives me any courage."

"And then, my beauty," reassured the good grandmother, kissing her granddaughter, "soon you'll be better, and you'll be cured... yes, I'm sure of it... you'll be cured!"

"I'll be cured!" murmured the dying girl, lifting her eyes towards the heavens that already seemed to be calling her.

A discreet knock came from the door to the single modest bedroom in which these two victims of fate were living, in a worker's cottage on Rue Nollet.

"Who could have come to see us?" wondered the old woman.

"Perhaps it's him?" guessed the consumptive, with a gasp of hope.

"I'll open the door."

Madame Vernier, groping her way, headed towards the door, which she opened a crack.

"I beg your pardon, Madame, to disturb you like this," said a loud masculine voice. "I'm Colonel Richard."

"You! You came! At last!" Madeleine cried, pressing her hands together.

Chantecoq, his hat in his hand, entered a room... which revealed true misery, courage, and one who, not yet completely discouraged, was fighting to the end!

A feeling of deep pity engulfed the policeman at once on seeing this distress whose full extent he had guessed at a glance, as well as all the injustice.

Considering the two poor creatures with a tender gaze, the old lady with white hair and the invalid whose suffering, while ravaging her features, couldn't completely erase her beauty, the detective thought, "I was right to come. These two ladies can only have told the truth."

Madeleine Vernier replied, "So you are Colonel Richard?"

"Yes, Mademoiselle," replied the detective without hesitation.

"I've waited so long for you. You're finally here! I'm happy, so happy, because I'm doubtless going, just as I wrote to you, to spare you and your daughter from irreparable misfortune. But please sit down, Colonel."

Chantecoq, throughout the course of his police career, so replete with incidents and accidents of all kinds, had perhaps never felt such a strange emotion.

Indeed, he found it repugnant to play this farce out before the two women who were exuding such honesty, such truthfulness.

He almost regretted his curiosity, his insatiable desire to learn everything... and his loyalty was rebelling at a situation whose difficulties and importance he was reproaching himself for not having sufficiently foreseen.

Nevertheless, Chantecoq understood it was too late to back down and far too late to abandon his character.

And yet it was with a timid air that he sat down on the edge of a seat, while the grandmother remained on her feet, leaning on the back of the old armchair from which her granddaughter had not moved.

"Colonel," continued Madeleine, who, in the presence of the man whose coming she had desired so fiercely, seemed to have regained some temporary strength. "Colonel, I'll get straight to the point. Because I suppose you are as anxious to know... as I am anxious to speak."

"Certainly, Mademoiselle," said the detective, more and more embarrassed.

"I'm going to tell you a terrible secret," continued the young girl. "Just as I wrote to you, your honour, as well as

Mademoiselle Richard's future and happiness, are at stake...
I'm going to tell you by whom... and how.

"But first, Colonel, you must give me your word as a
French officer that after having drawn your personal profit
from the rigorously precise information that I'm about to
communicate to you in my grandmother's presence, you will
never reveal to anyone in the world, no matter whom, the
terrifying secret that my duty tells me I must entrust to you."

This time, Chantecoq was on the point of standing up
and shouting, "Mademoiselle, tell me no more. I can't
undertake the engagement that you're demanding of me..."

This was indeed because the ever more overwhelmed
detective was thinking, "This terrible confidence, uniquely
destined to be received by the unfortunate Colonel Richard,
do I have the right to hear it? It perhaps consists only of an
entirely intimate business, completely personal."

But he answered himself. "However, on the other hand,
isn't it above all his memory, isn't it above all to protect his
daughter from a mysterious danger which threatens her that
I'm acting? How delicate all this is... difficult, even
anguishing!"

Understanding the struggle raging in her guest's mind,
though without guessing its cause, Mademoiselle Vernier
continued.

"I see that you hesitate, Colonel... and that's very natural.
A man such as you must not care to give his word without
knowing much about why. Well, I shall free you from all
scruples."

And with a tone of such gravity that she managed to
plunge the detective into a discomfort such as he'd never yet
experienced, the consumptive declared, "If I impose such
rigorous conditions upon you, it's because the wretch I'm

106

about to, if you allow me, unmask for you, belongs to a whole association of wrongdoers which, if an indiscretion was committed, would immediately know from where the leak had come and wouldn't hesitate to murder, my grandmother and I."

At those words which opened a whole new horizon to him, Chantecoq ceased to procrastinate.

Those words above all: *a whole association of wrongdoers* were enough to banish all misgivings, any reticence from his mind.

The policeman regained his total self-control.

Stifling all sentimentality which appeared to him at that moment like a guilty weakness, determined to see through to the end a mission he considered to be more than his professional duty, but a sacred task of sorts, he said in a firm and resolved voice, " Mademoiselle, that's understood! You have my word of honour. You can tell me everything in complete security."

"Thank you, Colonel," the two ladies said simultaneously, apparently suddenly delivered from the most piercing of anxieties.

Then, transfigured, reborn, as though the implacable sickness from which she suffered had just abandoned her, Mademoiselle Vernier continued.

"Colonel... I learned... I can't tell you how, because I also had to swear, myself. Anyway, I know, and this is the main thing, that Mademoiselle your daughter was sought in marriage by Monsieur Louis Marois, an industrialist from Maubeuge, and that, without taking a final decision on the matter, you were inclined to take a favourable view of a union which seemed certain to assure a happy and shining future for your child."

Chantecoq, highly intrigued, believed he ought to nod in affirmation.

The young girl continued. "Now, this Monsieur Marois… is quite simply a German spy."

"What are you saying?" the detective exclaimed, carried away by emotion.

"I'm saying that the wretch, who's been passing himself off as an industrialist… is really called Ulrich von Herfeld, and that he's a Captain in the Prussian army."

"How did you come across such a secret?"

With a simple tone and incomparable nobility, the consumptive revealed, "I too, almost became his wife."

"You!"

"Yes, me, Colonel!"

"Speak! Tell me everything!" Chantecoq, carried away, couldn't help himself from shouting out.

14 A BROKEN HEART

While her grandmother, silent and apparently crushed under the blow of the sharpest pain, let her tears flow freely, Madeleine Vernier continued, growing ever more animated.

"Don't think, Colonel, that I'm obeying some desire for vengeance! No, the rest of my account will show you to what extent I am far from such feelings.

"Two years ago, I knew that man in Lille, where, after the death of my parents, I'd established myself as a piano teacher, with my dear grandmother.

"Little by little, with that tireless obstinacy common to people of his race, Marois, or rather von Herfeld succeeded in introducing himself into our intimate circle.

"With what end? I believe he was truly in love with me.

"He had very soft features, very affectionate...

"Not only was he very charming with regard to me; but he was so considerate and full of attention towards grandmother, offering to take her to a specialist who would treat her poor eyes which were already under threat; in brief, he showed himself to be so simple, so good, so devoted, that I had an infinite regard for him.

"He said he was without family, without any real affection, almost alone in the world. So, gradually, I felt myself drawn to him by feelings of very real friendship, of irresistible trust, so much so that when one evening, very emotional, at least in appearance - but I repeat this, he then appeared sincere - he alluded to a union between us, I dropped my hand into his own.

"The following day, we exchanged our definitive promises. Our marriage was set for spring, that's to say three months away, my fiancé having to make a trip to Russia where he claimed to have substantial industrial interests.

"We left with him in his automobile. No need to tell you that, throughout the journey, he was in an increasing hurry. Yes, yes, I'm certain, he loved me.

"In Paris, we each went to a separate hotel. We had already done quite a lot of shopping together. No need to tell you he had showered me with gifts... and that, not for a moment had he ceased to assure me that, henceforth, his life's sole aim was to make me the happiest of women... when, one morning, he seemed worried, preoccupied. He had, he said, received a telegram which forced him to bring forward his trip by one week, and he asked permission to leave the next morning for Saint Petersburg, where his interests were calling him with all haste.

"I confess I felt a certain sorrow at this. I feel no shame in declaring, I was more and more attached to that man; and, it's horrible to say, the feeling of friendship he inspired in me at first was gradually transformed, without me even being fully aware, into pure and very real love."

"Poor darling," Madame Vernier observed sorrowfully, passing her handkerchief across her poor face which was wet with tears.

"Grandmother, sit down, please," Madeleine invited her.

Then Chantecoq, gently, took the blind woman by the arm and led her to another armchair, just as old and just as ruined as that occupied by the consumptive.

She, more and more galvanised by the effort that she was imposing upon herself, waited until the fake Colonel resumed his place and, with a melancholy accent which, better than anything expressed her renunciation of all joy in this world, the unhappy child continued.

"A little more patience, Colonel, I'm getting to the tragic conclusion of our adventure.

"Before separating from my fiancé for some time, I wanted to offer him a pleasant surprise.

"I sat in secret for a portrait with a great photographer, and I wanted to give it to him on the eve of his departure. The moment had come, then…

"I went to buy a pretty frame on Avenue de l'Opéra. I still see the shop. Then, knowing my fiancé needed to do some shopping in the morning, I went to his hotel and, with the help of a generous tip, I obtained authorisation to enter his room with grandmother, so much more easily because we'd both often been seen with him, and I was known to everyone as his fiancée.

"I unwrapped my little parcel, and I was preparing to hang the frame on the chimney when, suddenly, a slightly puerile idea came into my head. I'd just spotted, on a trestle table, in a bay window, a rather large suitcase, whose straps were not yet buckled…

111

"At once I thought, 'I'll slip my portrait in there, hide it among his clothes, and, when my fiancé reaches the end of his journey, he'll find me there, right next to him.'"

"A charming thought!" said Chantecoq, who was following Mademoiselle Vernier's account with ever greater attention.

She replied at once. "A providential thought, as you're about to learn, Colonel. At first, I hit a snag. The suitcase was locked.

"What to do? I recalled I had brought my keyring in my handbag. Despite grandmother feeling I was being most indiscreet, pushed by a mysterious, incomprehensible force, I tried my smallest keys successively in the lock. One of them was just the right shape, the suitcase opened.

"Then I gave a cry of stupefaction. I thought I was dreaming. In one of the compartments, I saw the carefully folded uniform of a German officer. A cry escaped my lips."

And as Madeleine, as though still feeling the blow of that unexpected vision, stopped to catch her breath, Madame Vernier murmured in a trembling voice, "That cry, I'll remember it forever!"

The invalid, in haste to finish, because she felt from the irritation in her chest that the coughing fits were about to seize her again, but supported by the obstinate will of getting to the end of her task, continued with superhuman courage.

"I stayed there, petrified, my eyes fixed on the dark tunic, the pointed helmet. Overwhelmed by an irresistible desire to know the full truth, I grabbed the helmet, I turned it over...

"Inside was written a name in golden letters: *Captain Ulrich von Herfeld*. I was transfixed!

"Suddenly, it dawned on me. The man I was going to marry was a German spy! I crashed to the floor in a dead faint! When I came round, I was lying on a bed. Grandmother was leaning over me, covering me with kisses. It was those maternal caresses which had awoken me.

"But nearby stood a man, whom I didn't recognise at once, his face was so twisted with an expression of terrible rage. 'Madeleine,' he said, 'what have you done?'

"Then the atrocious, dreadful reality appeared to me. I made no answer. Doubtless, my fiancé read in my eyes what was going on within me, my shattered love, transforming to contempt and even hatred for he who had misled me so odiously and, who knows, in marrying me was perhaps trying to make me his accomplice.

"Indeed, he continued immediately, in a hoarse, evil voice, that I didn't recognise from him. 'Madeleine, you've discovered a terrible secret. At this moment, you hold my fate in your hands. One word from you, and I'm lost!'

"Giving into my twice-outraged Frenchwoman's indignation, with an instinctive, irrational gesture, I was already reaching for the electric buzzer placed on the wall next to the bed... when, with startling speed, Monsieur Marois, or rather Captain von Herfeld, drew his revolver on me, saying, in a voice that I'll never forget, 'Madeleine, I loved you and I love you still. But if you call out, I'll blow your brains out!'

"Scoundrel!" said Chantecoq through gritted teeth.

Then with a voice filled with incomparable heroism, Mademoiselle Vernier said simply, "I was about to call all the same! But grandmother rushed to the wretch's feet, begging him to spare me, promising him, swearing to him that I would hold my tongue, imploring me, me too, begging me to keep quiet, assuring me with heartbreaking sobs that she wouldn't outlive me for more than a minute...

113

"My arm fell back on the bed. Coldly, the German officer replaced his revolver in its holster. 'Well done,' he said fiercely. 'If you had called, I would have killed both of you! I'll spare you, but remember this: I forbid you to return to Lille. Henceforth, you'll live in Paris. I warn you that you will be subject, without you ever being aware of it, to incessant surveillance. If ever I'm discovered… I'll know it was because of you. That same evening, both of you will die.'

"He added with a sort of wild strength, 'Because we're very strong… stronger than you could possibly imagine.' And the bandit dared to conclude, 'As the price of your silence, you'll receive a sum of five hundred francs each month.'"

"'Stop!' I cried. I was so outraged by this man's revolting cynicism that for the second time my hand was about to move towards the wall. Yes, I preferred death to such shame.

"But… my eyes met those of my grandmother. I read in them such dreadful distress… which was begging me so hard to live… that I faltered, I was a coward… I committed a crime against my country for which I will never forgive myself, a crime for which I'm dying, and I answered:

"'Don't worry, Monsieur. We won't say anything, neither my grandmother or I. We'll stay in Paris as you demand. As to your money, keep it. Don't impose on us the shame of accepting such dishonourable charity from you.'

"'Please yourself,' said Captain von Herfeld, who added, 'I'm going to leave this hotel at once. You will stay in this room for half an hour. Then, you can do whatever you want on the condition, I repeat, that you don't leave the capital.'

"Then, without saying another word, while grandmother and I were weeping in each other's arms, quite calmly, the German officer shut his suitcase and went to the door. In the doorway, he turned back to say again to us, 'Never forget that your lives depend on my security. Farewell!'

"He vanished. I've not seen that man since. Since that terrible scene, you can't imagine what our lives have been like, my grandmother and I. We've always felt a perpetual, continual, mysterious surveillance weighing down on us. Although we obeyed that wretch's injunctions - the great despair of my life - we no longer enjoy a moment's peace.

"Grandmother soon lost her sight completely. And then, life was so hard! Piano lessons, even for a franc, for fifty centimes, were becoming ever rarer.

"Broken with fatigue, chewed up with remorse, I fell ill. So I was on the point of speaking. This secret was choking me. I knew that von Herfeld had returned to Mauberge, that he was living there in high esteem, respected by everyone, continuing in the shadow of his dreadful work.

"Oh! Yes, more than twenty times I wanted to find a policeman. But when I saw my poor old grandmother, when I felt her draw me into her arms... all my courage failed, I was continuing to be cowardly through family duty, and I kept quiet. I would doubtless have held my tongue to the last, if I hadn't learned that you were on the point of giving your daughter to this monster.

"So, this time, it was my grandmother who said, 'Speak! Perhaps he'll kill both of us! But we can't allow such a crime!'"

"Poor ladies!" Chantecoq said simply, his eyes also full of tears.

Then, fighting down the emotion which was disturbing him, the detective continued. "From the bottom of my heart, Mademoiselle, I thank you. You've just carried out an act which must help you forget the remorse for a very excusable failure! Because you who stared death in the face, you can only be pardoned for not wanting to sacrifice she who, through her touching generosity and her admirable tenderness, represented everything on earth for you, just as she, the venerable creature, refused to allow you to perish, you who are everything in this world for her."

"Thank you, Colonel," said Mademoiselle Vernier, holding out her emaciated hand to the detective, who took hold of it and brought it respectfully to his lips.

"Oh! Yes, thank you, Monsieur..." repeated the blind woman, who, in a broken, dejected voice, added, "I too have suffered so much."

"Well, ladies," replied the detective, "this dreadful existence you've been leading for the last two years is about to end. Because I won't abandon you until I've delivered you, until I've torn you from the invisible trap of which you've been the victims.

"So, once I have you both safely stowed, when you'll have nothing more to fear from those scoundrels, who work from the shadows to ruin our nation, I'll ask you to release me from the oath that you demanded from me, so that, quickly, I can in a single vengeful action, punish your, and my country's tormentor."

At those words, Madeleine Vernier, with a supreme effort, stood up.

Her whole body was shivering with the spirit of the noblest sacrifice. "Colonel! Colonel!" she cried, "I release you from your promise this very instant. Yes, yes, the nation! Grandmother, we must! Even though... yes... yes, we must!"

Approaching her grandmother at a hesitant pace, moving with difficulty, Madeleine Vernier gasped, "We delayed too long! We've been guilty, so guilty. But we're only two women, and we each feared for the other! We love each other so much, so much! You understand, don't you?"

"Didn't I already say I forgave you!" said the detective, with a tone full of boundless compassion.

Then, delirious, the consumptive, standing close to her grandmother, whose arms she had taken gently, and wrapped them maternally around her waist, continued, ever more exultantly,

"You're so kind. Ah! How happy I am to have warned you in time. Your daughter will escape this monster. And France too must escape him. You'll have him arrested, aren't you? Because now I'm no longer afraid! I don't fear him! He can kill me. I'll be happy to die, yes, very happy indeed.

"But save grandmother, save her, in the name of heaven, Colonel... Colonel!"

The dying woman said nothing more.

Blood flowed from her mouth.

With a final supreme effort, she remained standing... for the three seconds necessary for Chantecoq to catch her in his arms.

Her head rolled back against his shoulder.

A faint glimmer of light died in her eyes, while a barely perceptible breath slipped from her bloody lips.

"Madeleine!" called the blind woman, who feared she understood. "Madeleine! My beloved girl, my darling child!"

Her searching, groping hand, found Chantecoq who, with a strong arm, was holding up the dead woman.

"Is it over?" she murmured. "It is finished?"

His throat hoarse, his reason overwhelmed by the dreadful drama unfolding in that attic, the detective could only say weakly, "Madame!"

117

Then, letting out a terrible cry, the grandmother collapsed to the ground, also mortally stricken, and repeated in a half-moan, "It's over!"

"It's over for you, you poor martyrs..." cried Chantecoq, "but for me, this is just the beginning!"

15 FIRST KISS

"I assure you it was him, I saw him, I recognised him. No! Lieutenant, I'm not the victim of a hallucination, it was indeed my father who was there, before me, it was really him."

And the Colonel's daughter, gasping with emotion, let herself fall back on a sofa, her eyes wild, as if she was still glimpsing the tragic vision she had experienced the night before.

Raymond Vallier, enslaved by the promise he'd made, tried his best to mislead the young girl.

"I assure you, Mademoiselle Yvonne," he said, "that you're mistaken."

"No, no," the young girl was obstinate. "I remember very well. After a long sleepless night, I ended up falling into a feverish, agitated sleep, when I woke with a start. I was dreaming of my father. I saw him surrounded by enemies ready to strike him down. He called me to his aid…"

"You see…"

"Let me finish, Lieutenant, I beg you."

And with the deepest conviction, the pretty creature continued.

"I got up. With an instinctive movement, without really knowing what I was doing, I ran to the window. I saw a light in the office. Quickly, I threw a shawl over my shoulders. I went down to the courtyard. Then I noticed, keeping close to the buildings, as though trying to stay out of sight, a man of the same stature and gait as my father.

"In a flash I was near him. By the light of the moon which was enveloping him, although he was trying to hide his face, I recognised him, I'm certain of it. I was awake, properly awake, completely conscious of what was going on around me. I therefore couldn't be mistaken on this point and even should I live a hundred years, I'll still see him. It was him, it was really him…

"As I held out my arms to him, as I called to him, I had the very clear impression that he was trying to avoid me, that he was fleeing from me. Then I felt such a painful shock inside me, so terrible that I fell into a faint and it seemed to me that I was dying."

Her face wet with tears, her chest heaving with sobs, Yvonne Richard couldn't stop repeating in a broken voice, "My father, my poor father!"

As for Lieutenant Vallier, he watched her with eyes full of tender compassion and intense love.

He thought, "Ah! Why did the Colonel forbid me so formally, so absolutely, from telling his daughter that he's still alive? Why, finding himself face to face with her, did he steal away from her embrace instead of reassuring her with one word, thereby putting an end to the atrocious sorrow which crushes her? Why did he leave her in the cruellest doubt, in the most dreadful equivocation?"

But the young officer felt that by remaining silent, it was tantamount to confessing to the young girl that he too had seen her father.

Fundamentally honest, loyal above all to the promise he'd made, Raymond Vallier, by adopting such an attitude, would believe himself guilty of the worst act of cowardice, the lowest hypocrisy.

Because, the more he thought about it, the more he thought, "I think I know Colonel Richard quite well. I know all the affection he has for his daughter. Very well! For him to act in this way, ready to shatter her hopes further, he must have the most powerful motives.

"However, he permitted me to glimpse those motives, when he cried, 'For the honour of my name, for the glory of the nation!' Therefore, more than ever, silence is imposed upon me."

And, aloud, he replied in an emotional voice, full of kindness and charm. "Yvonne, I beg you, be calm. Chase from your brain all these thoughts which are afflicting and disturbing it."

"But what about you?" asked the young girl, with a tone that revealed persistent doubt. "Didn't you see anything, hear anything?"

"Yes, I heard your terrible scream. I was working in my office, so I came running at once."

"And you found me alone?"

"Completely alone, lying on the ground, unconscious."

"Truly, my dear Raymond?"

"Truly, my lovely Yvonne."

"Ah! My friend, my friend, how unhappy I am!"

Seeking to calm down, to regain control of her nerves, the industrialist's daughter said, "I so much want to believe you,

121

but I still see him… still… Oh! Wait, I don't know any more. It seems to me that misery gathers around us, and I'll never see my father again."

"Yvonne, don't say such a thing!"

"This Monsieur Dalibert who ought to have given us some news so promptly? You see, we've not received anything yet."

"Patience!"

"After all, that man must have appeared very wise, and very serious, we don't know him."

"He's a State engineer!"

"Why was he interested in my father?"

"First because he seemed to me to be a brave man; then, he was in contact with the Colonel, and himself, through his functions…"

"Oh! Hold on!" Yvonne interrupted, no longer capable of controlling her reactions, "I'm beginning to doubt everything, even Providence."

"And me… quite the opposite," affirmed the young officer forcefully, "I have more faith in it than ever before."

And giving his voice an inflection of endless affection, Raymond Vallier added, "Wasn't I there? And you know how much I love you!"

"I love you too."

"Oh! My dear Yvonne, shouldn't those words which just escaped our lips be enough to bring us hope?"

"My friend…"

"And then, I've an idea - what am I saying, I'm certain - the good times will return, and perhaps sooner than you think! One has these intuitions. It's called having faith. And faith in love, isn't that the greatest, most beautiful and most powerful thing in the world? Be assured then, my beloved, because I can now call you that, can't I?"

"More than ever!"

"Yes, my beloved, have no fear, we'll be happy, very happy together."

"Together?"

"Always together!"

Yvonne Richard, recovering all her bravery, cried out, with a tone full of superb willpower, "Raymond, you're right, we can't let ourselves be beaten down! When one loves like we love, when one decides to follow the same path hand in hand, to rejoice from the same joys and to suffer the same pains, one is strong... what am I saying? One is strongest of all."

With sudden and triumphant energy, the Colonel's daughter added, "Henceforth, whatever should happen, it's to you, my love, my true love, that I pledge my fate, and offer my whole life!"

"How happy I am to hear you talking like this," cried the Lieutenant, transfigured with joy, "and you are so beautiful... Ah! How I love you!"

Spontaneously, the couple held hands.

In a gesture full of the most exquisite chastity, Yvonne Richard offered her forehead to the lieutenant's lips who, for the first time, planted a long kiss there, a kiss of betrothal, which sealed forever love's most sacred promises.

Both, then, looked at each other in silence. Oh! Yes, how they loved each other.

These two beings so young, so attractive, and so vibrant with matching sentiments of bravery and generosity, seemed to have been created for each other.

Their love was revealed to be immense and pure, exempt from the petty calculations which preside all too often over marriages.

They already represented the ideal couple. He, the husband who was hard-working, energetic, loyal, gifted with those luminous qualities which light the way on life's path which becomes that of happiness... she, the wife, in the most adorable and poetic sense of the word, tirelessly devoted companion, scattering flowers with a smile on the path they were both travelling!

Remembering his duty, the young officer continued, almost shyly. "My dear Yvonne, I beg your pardon a thousand times, but I've been summoned to the Arsenal, at three o'clock. It's now half-past two, and I'm afraid of arriving late."

"Oh! Yes, go! My love!" the Colonel's daughter ushered him towards the door. "I'd hate to be the cause of any negligence in your service."

"Then goodbye, Yvonne, and I'll see you soon, shan't I?"

"Always!"

Left alone, Yvonne Richard was still pensive.

Her face which had lit up under her beloved's kiss darkened gradually.

Her tears, halted for a moment, again began to flow.

Then falling back on the sofa, the poor child cried, "Father! My dear Father! Raymond may say... I feel I'll never see him again!"

16 A PECULIAR VISIT

How long did Yvonne remain like that, prostrate, sobbing, in her daughterly sorrow? Two hours, three hours?

Even she herself would have had trouble saying.

So it was that she was torn from her reverie by a knock at her door.

"Come in!" she said mechanically.

The gentle Françoise appeared.

"Oh! My poor lady," she cried, "here you are again in tears."

Urgently, maternally, the brave servant continued. "If this goes on you're surely going to fall ill. You mustn't get yourself into such a state."

With disarming naivety, the excellent girl added, "That's not going to bring your father back."

"That's true," acknowledged Yvonne, "I was wrong to let everything get on top of me."

"Oh yes, you must take care of yourself, and who's to say he's not going to come back? This very evening, perhaps? Come, my little lady, dry your eyes. Loving you so much, it pains me to see you like this. I, who am preparing such a lovely little dinner for you, with nothing but the things you love, to convince you to eat. Because it's soon going to be three days that you've taken nothing, and that's not reasonable…"

"My dear Françoise," sighed the Colonel's daughter sadly. "If you only knew how grateful I am to you for all your kindness towards me!"

"Isn't that only natural? No more mother, nothing but distant parents…"

"Geographically and sentimentally…" Yvonne said in a melancholy tone.

"Isn't it only fair," declared the brave creature, "that I love you so much that I cut myself into four to pamper you and console you?"

And without any afterthoughts, Françoise added, "There's also Lieutenant Vallier, who seems to love you dearly. I like him a lot, that boy."

"Françoise," interrupted Yvonne, whose face was coloured with a slight blush… "Go and see if there are any letters in the box."

"I just went to check, Mademoiselle, there weren't any…"

Then the old maid gave a start, and cried out, "In fact, yes, now I think of it! There was something… oh! Not a letter… a visitor for Mademoiselle."

"A visitor for me?"

"Yes, a gentleman, with a very proper air, who has already come several times. I showed him into the dining room, and I forgot all about him. Ah! Where did I put my head, then?"

Heading towards the door, Françoise asked, "Should I show him in?"

"Did he give you his name?"

"No, but he handed me his card. Ah! Now what did I do with that? I'm definitely losing my marbles. Ah! There it is, in my apron pocket."

The brave girl held out a slim calling card to Yvonne, who took it and read,

Louis MAROIS
Industrialist, Maubeuge
Would be obliged to Mademoiselle Yvonne Richard, for whom he has deep concerns, if she would receive him, if only for a few minutes, in respectful sympathy, because he has a very important communication for her.

Yvonne's first reaction was to cry out, "No way!"

Indeed, aware of the first approaches this man had attempted towards her father, the indifference he had inspired in her up to then had been transformed into a kind of aversion, justified by the deep love that she had pledged to Lieutenant Vallier.

Wasn't it Marois who had succeeded, by arguing with the man whom her heart had chosen and by capturing the Colonel's good graces, to further increase the obstacle which opposed the realisation of a wish which was henceforth her entire life?

For her, wasn't he henceforth the enemy?

And yet, a thought crossed her mind.

Yvonne Richard thought, "This Marois may have some useful information for me on the subject of my father. However painful it may be for me to receive him, I've no right to banish him."

Then, aloud, she decided, "Françoise, I'm going up to my bedroom for a moment. Because I can't receive visitors with red eyes. Once I've left, show this gentleman into the lounge and ask him to wait a few moments for me."

"Very good, Mademoiselle."

The young girl, intrigued by this rather unexpected visit, reached the hallway, and disappeared upstairs.

Carrying out her mistress's instructions, Françoise returned to the dining room, announcing to the visitor in that familiar tone of which she'd never been able to rid herself, "Come with me, Monsieur, Mademoiselle will receive you."

Captain von Herfeld, with an appearance that was more vigorous than it was distinguished, but dressed absolutely correctly in his tailored frock coat, followed the servant who led him into the lounge saying, "If you would just wait here a minute, Mademoiselle won't be long."

Discreetly, Françoise withdrew… while the visitor took a deep breath, muttering in the purest German ever spoken by a Professor of Bonn or Heidelberg university, "Finally, here I am!"

Then, with his snooping instincts, that irresistible need to inform oneself which characterises all Germans, especially when acting as a spy, von Herfeld began to inspect the room.

At first his attention was drawn to a beautiful eighteenth century clock, a family heirloom.

He looked at it for some time with an envious air.

Then his eyes flitted towards a portrait of Colonel Richard, to which he accorded only a contemptuous shrug of his shoulders.

But a photograph of Yvonne drew his attention for longer.

With a villainous smile, he mumbled, still in German, "They're all pretty, these French girls… and her in particular."

Then he added, "With Mademoiselle Richard, I won't let myself be caught like with the other one. She'll be my wife, I want her!"

A slight sound brought him back to reality.

Yvonne Richard, the touchingly adorable beauty, enveloped in an atmosphere of sadness which further added to her charm, was quietly entering the lounge.

"Mademoiselle," began the fake industrialist, in pure French this time, and with a tone of the most perfect deference, "Mademoiselle, please forgive me if I have forced your door in any way. But I heard sad news, and I hastened to come running, not only to express my most respectful devotion, but further to offer you... my very humble services."

"Monsieur," replied the Colonel's daughter, surprised and even resentful at this approach. "I can only thank you for your kindness... but... forgive me for being astonished. Having only rarely had the opportunity to meet you, I ask myself why your kindness with regards to me judges it appropriate to manifest itself in this fashion, without my having solicited it in the slightest."

In no way deterred by that rather chilly riposte, the fake industrialist replied in a gentle tone which made a peculiar contrast with his brutal appearance. "I learned about the dreadful event."

"What do you mean?" Mademoiselle Richard asked.

"The disappearance of Colonel..."

"I don't understand."

"Of course, Mademoiselle, it's quite natural that you would want to keep hidden such a terrible thing. But, unfortunately, the mystery is beginning to become clear. The proof of it is in this newspaper article I am taking the liberty of communicating to you, and which will not fail, I'm sure, to justify my presence at your side."

While speaking these words, von Herfeld had taken from his pocket an issue of a large regional daily newspaper and, unfolding it, he put it before the young girl's eyes, while pointing out to her a passage which was underlined in blue pencil.

More and more stupefied, Lieutenant Vallier's fiancée read the following:

Rumours are starting to be whispered, very quietly, about the peculiar disappearance of one of the superior officers at the Douai garrison, Colonel R… specially charged with the technical direction of one of the most important establishments for our national defence.

A rather troubling detail has emerged: the immediate entourage of this officer, whose career, we hasten to declare, has been glorious and his private life extremely worthy, have neglected to alert the civilian and military authorities of an absence which can not be explained.

Could they fear a scandal?

While the young girl was reading this titbit, she felt her face grow pale.

The last sentence which was so threatening in its laconicism, *'Could they fear a scandal?'* managed to trouble her deeply.

"Monsieur," she said to Marois, returning the newspaper to him with a shaking hand, "I don't really understand. I don't even see…"

She stopped, choked with emotion.

17 A BOUNDER

Still in the same gentle voice, von Herfeld answered her.

"Mademoiselle, you must have noticed that it's talking about your father, as I myself noticed."

As Yvonne Richard kept quiet, the officer - or rather the German spy - continued, in a tone to which he tried to lend the expression of the most affectionate devotion, of absolute respect.

"You really were wrong, Mademoiselle, not to trust me. Although from your face... sorry, from the traces of tears I notice in your eyes, I guess that you're unhappy, very unhappy. Well! Allow me to advise you, to help you. Alone in the world, young, inexperienced, it's completely natural that in the face of an event that could never have been foreseen, you've lost your head a little, and neglected the most elementary precautions that must always be taken in such cases. Accept that, in these very painful circumstances, I'm better than your guide, your friend..."

Regaining control to the point of pushing her sorrow deep down within herself, Yvonne replied, "I greatly regret, Monsieur, that I'm unable to accept your offers."

"Why's that, then?" asked the German with a certain sharpness.

Then with a coldness that verged on disdain, the Colonel's daughter, raising her head proudly, declared, "Because I don't know you."

At those words, Captain von Herfeld gave a genuine start of shock.

"What! Mademoiselle," he said, forcing himself to remain calm. "What, you don't know me? I understand the challenge you're enduring at the moment is troubling you to the point of affecting your memory. But Mademoiselle, allow me to remind you, with all the deference that I owe you, that we've often met through mutual friends, most recently in Lille, at tea with General de Ricourt d'Avrigny, that I even had the honour of receiving you at my table with Colonel Richard, and that finally, he... oh! I beg your pardon a thousand times, but it was you who forced me to be precise... no, I'll stop. I would be too afraid of crossing you, of offending you, while to the contrary, my whole being lives with only one goal, one thought, to devote myself to you!

"Don't repulse me, I beg you. You would be wrong, so wrong. I can be useful to you, very useful.

"Certainly I hope with all my heart that the disappearance of brave Colonel Richard, for whom I have such friendship and esteem, is only of short duration, and this remarkable officer will soon resume his place at his post and in his home.

"I'll add that I've a private and profound conviction that, whatever happens, the scandal to which this newspaper

132

refs so clumsily and imprudently, is impossible. Your father is one of those soldiers who is fearless and beyond reproach, and should remain above all suspicion.

"However, I thought that you must be sad, anxious, and that's why I came to you with my hand held out loyally."

And without appearing to notice the true repulsion painted on the young girl's face, von Herfeld, who was not ceasing to devour her with an ardent and covetous gaze, dared to conclude:

"You are wrong to offer me disdain, Mademoiselle Yvonne, because I declare, affirm, and swear to you, that there isn't another man on the face of the planet who could be more powerfully, eternally attached to you."

Still in control of her emotions, but no less distant, Colonel Richard's daughter replied. "Monsieur, it would be ingracious of me not to thank you for the offer of a devotion that I choose to believe is… disinterested."

"Oh! Entirely, Mademoiselle."

"But, with a frankness of which I have made one of my guiding principles, permit me to answer you that I can not accept it."

"Truly!"

"And that's for two reasons."

"Oh! What are they?"

"First, as you said yourself, my father's absence is doubtless temporary and *whatever happens* - I use your own expression - his name shines with a light too pure to be tainted by calumny."

"Certainly, Mademoiselle… I am and I will always be the first to proclaim it."

"As to the second reason…"

"Oh! Yes, tell me quickly, very quickly."

Then, with an accent which ought to have imposed eternal silence on the rogue and oaf that was Captain von Herfelt, Lieutenant Vallier's fiancée cried out, "I refuse to believe, Monsieur, that you've not already guessed."

"Oh! Mademoiselle, I assure you I have no idea what you mean."

"Allow me to be frankly astonished at that."

"And allow me to ask you immediately to tell me precisely…"

"So be it! I prefer that there shouldn't be any misunderstanding between us."

Superbly resolved and strong, Yvonne Richard declared, "Some time ago, Monsieur Marois, you asked my father for my hand."

"Yes, Mademoiselle."

"How did he answer you?"

"That, for his part, he saw no obstacles to a project which gave him great personal satisfaction. He even added a few words with regard to me which were far too flattering for me to repeat."

"He didn't add anything else?"

"I don't recall anything."

"Let's see, search your memories… you can't find anything? Very well, I'll tell you. My father added that he would make me aware of your request."

"Naturally…"

"And he would give you a response after giving me all the time necessary to reflect upon it."

"Nothing more proper than that."

"Well, Monsieur Marois, that response, I'll give it to you myself. It's clear and definitive. I will never be your wife!"

"Mademoiselle Yvonne!" von Herfeld said, in a cry where there was something close to despair.

"Don't judge me for speaking with such sharpness," continued Yvonne. "I feel that in such cases it's better to get straight to the point, and it would have been unworthy of me to allow the slightest illusion to remain in you."

"Mademoiselle!" insisted the fake industrialist. "I can't believe that your decision is irrevocable."

"Then you are mistaken… Monsieur."

"I love you!"

"I regret to be obliged to cause you any pain; but I don't love you, and I never will."

"No! No! That's impossible!" said von Herfeld in a thick voice.

"Monsieur, don't force me to insist on ending this visit which is extremely painful for me."

"I beg you to let me plead my cause!"

"It was lost in advance! Withdraw, Monsieur."

"Not before having made one final effort, to soften you."

And the German officer, the spy, the traitor, whether he was playing an atrocious farce, or whether he really was attracted, conquered, subjugated by the truly supernatural charm which the young girl exuded, fell to his knees.

"Have you not thought of the happy life I can offer you, then? I am rich, I may become even richer and I love you to such a point that nothing will be too fine for you, and my sovereign joy will be to make you the happiest of women."

"I'm not for sale!" countered Yvonne, more and more sickened by the attitude and words of he who was humiliating himself before her in this fashion.

But, tenacious to the last, von Herfeld continued. "I expressed myself badly. I don't know any more, I meant to say..."

"Enough!" the Colonel's daughter interrupted with authority.

And while, his eyes haggard, his arms stretched out in front, the wretch tried again to stammer some vague words, superb with wrath, the Colonel's daughter shouted.

"What's all this! Monsieur Marois, you choose the moment where I'm alone, in anguish and in tears, to come and speak to me of love! When, with a feeling of loyalty to which you ought to have inclined, I declare that I will never be your wife, instead of retiring discreetly, nobly, you persist in an attitude which would be completely odious, if it wasn't simply ridiculous!"

"Mademoiselle, I beg you, don't oppress me like this," von Herfeld still dared to say in a voice which had become hoarse and unpleasant.

"Get out!"

"One word... one single word?"

"Get out, I tell you!"

The lounge door opened loudly.

Lieutenant Vallier, grabbing the fake Marois by the arm, forced him to stand... then, without giving him time to recover from his surprise, with a steely grip, he pushed him rudely towards the door, ordering him, in one of those commanding tones which makes the most obstinate, audacious, reckless wills obey. "Yes! Get out! And never set foot here again!"

"Ah, who are you then?" the teutonic Captain dared to say, foaming with rage.

Proudly, the French officer retorted. "I'm a gallant man who's ready to punish you each time that you give him the opportunity."

"We shall see, Lieutenant Vallier," threatened von Herfeld, nevertheless prudently stepping outside.

"Whenever and wherever you like, Monsieur Louis Marois," said the artillery Lieutenant, whose firm gaze burned with all his energy.

Vallier returned to his fiancée, who was still in the grip of the emotion provoked by the insolent approach of he whom she considered to be an uneducated and heartless industrialist. Meanwhile, the German spy, crossing the powder mill's courtyard, rasped, "She will be mine, despite him… and despite her!"

And as a criminal gleam lit up his eyes, he added, "As to you, accursed Frenchman, you just signed your own death sentence!"

18 FRÉGOLI

Monsieur Aubry was beginning to worry.

It had been, indeed, more than three full hours since Chantecoq had left.

Knowing the detective well, he didn't fail to think, "For him to be so delayed, something serious must have occurred... very serious! Just as long as he hasn't fallen into some trap organised by those accursed German spies, for whom he is the *bête noire*! I'd perhaps do well to go and see.

"But he'd judge me for that, because he doesn't like it when people interfere with his business."

However the fears of the famous inventor of the combat aircraft and Explosive Z were about to be dispelled.

He heard the sound of keys turning in a lock. It was Chantecoq, who was still in the guise of Colonel Richard.

"Well, my friend, did all go as well as you hoped?" the great scholar asked eagerly.

"Yes, very well..." the bloodhound replied laconically.

Jean Aubry would never have questioned his friend further, not for all the world.

Because from the tone of his voice, he understood that the detective was not in the mood to share confidences.

And yet he said, "Imagine, I was beginning…"

"To get bored?" Chantecoq cut in with a smile.

"No! To worry."

"You were wrong; I was in no danger."

Then, in a tone imprinted at once with both gravitas and sadness, the policeman, approaching the inventor, said, "My dear Aubry, I just spent one of the most emotional hours of my life."

"Really?"

"I can't say any more than that, because it's necessary, before revealing what I just learned to anyone at all, that I verify the information I gathered in the course of a scene so tragic that, should I live a hundred years, will remain deeply engraved in my heart and in my memory."

"To be honest, you do still seem rather bewildered."

"When you find out!" said Chantecoq, resting his hand on his companion's shoulder, "Yes, when I feel I have the right to recount the truth to you, the whole truth, I'm sure you will share my emotion. I've been weeping, my friend… yes, weeping like an infant. That's happened to me only three times since I was ten years old.

"The first… was when I lost my son. The second, when I learned in Berlin that your admirable daughter, your dear and valiant Germaine, had been arrested by the German authorities."

"My friend!" said Jean Aubry, clasping the detective's hand with grateful effusion.

"The third, was today, when I found myself facing… but I can't, I must not tell you any more, at least for now."

And becoming himself again, that's to say full of energy, vigour and clear purpose, Chantecoq added, "May it suffice you to know that I've not wasted my time and I've done a good job. But now, I need to ask you something. That's to forget, temporarily at least, the letter I showed you."

"That's already done!"

"Thank you!"

Jean Aubry resisted the temptation to insist further. He knew his Chantecoq like the back of his hand. If he hadn't recounted his last expedition at length, it was doubtless because he had a serious reason to keep it secret.

In so acting, he was not only obeying that sentiment of discretion that was innate to him, but also an impulse from his own self-love which, as we already said, compelled him not to reveal the results of investigations, even to his closest friends, until he was entirely certain of success.

This method was sometimes very painful for those who, like the great scholar, were faithfully attached to him and who were always trembling at the thought that in the course of his life which was so adventurous and ceaselessly threatened by the enemy lurking in the shadows, were always afraid that he would be the victim of some fatal accident such as had already failed several times to claim his life.

But it was also a system that was excellent, even vital, from the point of view of professionalism and denoting on the part of he who was employing it, a great deal of prudence, tact, and wisdom.

Chantecoq continued. "Now, my dear friend, would you care to come with me to my bathroom? I've not finished bothering you yet."

"What a dreadful word you just spoke there!" Jean Aubry cried, all in a tone of friendly reproach. "You know very well that since your vital contribution to saving my daughter, we are friends to the end, to the death!"

"I know!"

"And then, after all, aren't we both attached to a common goal? The salvation and triumph of our dear nation?"

"That's true! You manufacture the engines which must bring us victory."

"And you, you thwart the scoundrels who have slipped among us in order to steal them."

"A close partnership, indissoluble..."

"You said it!"

"Too bad if I'm quoting you."

"All the better, as you'll never abuse it!"

While exchanging these words which demonstrated the understanding existing between these two minds which were so differently, but so powerfully gifted, at the same time as between two hearts beating with the same source of energy and courage. Chantecoq and Jean Aubry entered a room which was much larger than that of the world's most elegant society lady or the most acclaimed and coquettish actress.

One would have thought, indeed, that one was in the vast dressing room of a great actor, but unencumbered of those ornaments, portraits, drawings, the thousand and one souvenirs with which our great actors love to surround themselves, whether they evoke warm memories of their successes, or whether they remind them of fervent and precious friendships.

No, the bathroom, or rather the detective's dressing room contained only the numerous objects indispensable to he who was called upon to embody the most diverse characters, to pull off the most varied and unexpected transformations.

The inventor doubtless knew the place well, because he displayed no surprise upon entering.

While his friend pushed a switch, lighting rather brightly the room whose window and curtains were hermetically sealed, like in the middle of the night, he sat in a soft armchair and waited.

Chantecoq, after hanging his hat on a putter, went to sit in front of a mirror placed over a dressing table, on which was meticulously arranged everything necessary to disguise himself and which was lit by beams that converged skillfully from two electric lamps.

"Now," he said, "tell me a bit about your children."

"Gladly," said the inventor.

While with a dexterity which revealed great experience, and a speed verging on the prodigious, the detective removed his camouflage in order to become himself again; Jean Aubry began.

"I won't hide from you that I was deeply vexed when my son-in-law was sent on a mission to Maubeuge. So much more so as Germaine, and it's completely natural, insisted on following her husband. I find myself once again alone, really alone. My consolation is to visit them from time to time. Because they can hardly make trips themselves. Captain Evrard has a great deal to do."

"Still aviation?"

"Yes... it's marvellous what that boy manages to do. At the moment he's studying a completely new firing procedure which, while allowing aircraft pilots to maintain an elevation which keeps their machine sheltered from the enemy, will give the gunners accompanying the pilot the ability to regulate the launching of explosive bombs with mathematical regularity."

"You must have at least something to do with that," said Chantecoq in passing.

"My word, no! I fully intend to give my son-in-law full credit for that discovery."

"That's very interesting…"

"I don't need to tell you that my daughter follows her husband's work with passion. Despite everything I could do to dissuade her, she herself has become a dedicated aviator!"

"That doesn't surprise me!"

"She's even obtained her certificate. And in all the experiments the captain attempts, it's always she who accompanies him and who, more and more, takes the joystick or launches the projectiles. She's extraordinary!"

"Oh! That one!" exclaimed Chantecoq. "A long time ago I observed that she's carved from the wood, or rather the steel and even diamond from which heroines are built."

The bloodhound, whose face was entirely restored to its natural state, stood up, heading towards a huge wardrobe which he opened and which was full of all sorts of clothes, of uniforms, of all ranks and from all armies, and of the most diverse and assorted costumes, however they were all carefully arranged and meticulously labelled.

After having rid himself of the suit in which he was dressed, and having hung it from one of the wardrobe's hooks, the detective threw a furtive glance towards his guest; then he chose some black trousers which he put on immediately, and a frock coat of the same shade whose buttonhole bore a red ribbon and which he placed over the back of a chair.

Returning to his dressing table, he sat down, and while throwing frequent secretive glances in Jean Aubry's direction, he resumed a new and marvellous disguise.

The scholar, used to the policeman's transformations, didn't pay any attention at first.

He continued. "Yes, I'm proud to have such children. I don't need to tell you that they have formed the most charming and united couple that one could dream of."

"By Jove!" Chantecoq said approvingly, while dusting his face with a product called *deep police tinge*, invented entirely by him.

"Ah! It could be said that those two," continued the inventor, "have a fine horizon of happiness before them."

"They've certainly earned it!" said the detective, while lengthening and thickening his nose with the help of a special wax... which he modeled with extreme dexterity.

Then, choosing from the drawer of his table a wig and a greying moustache, he revolved the wheeled stool on which he was seated, in such a way as to turn his back squarely on his guest, whom he could still see very well in any case in the mirror before which he had placed himself.

Then, with the aid of very fine scissors, the bloodhound corrected and groomed the two hairpieces, trying them on, then removing them in order to modify them further.

Monsieur Aubry observed, "It seems to me, my dear friend, that you're engaged in a particularly complicated piece of work."

"Indeed," acknowledged Chantecoq, "what I'm attempting is rather tricky."

"Doubtless it's a very worthy person whose role you're going to play?"

"It's that of a genius."

"Simply that?"

"Simply that," stressed the bloodhound.

And in an almost joyful tone, he continued. "A man who has done immense service to his country and who will do greater services still in future. A man I admire with all my strength, a man whom you know in particular, but whom you certainly don't love as much as I do. A man, finally, who is not a million miles away from here... who I see... who I hear..."

And Chantecoq, turning back to his friend, suddenly cried out in triumph.

"Eh! Father Aubry! Do you think I've captured it, your mug?"

Explosive Z's inventor cried out, "It's me!"

The fact is that the policeman's 'work' had succeeded marvellously.

The most demanding eye, the most forewarned mind would have been incapable of discerning which of the two perfectly identical individuals was the true Jean Aubry.

It was more than just a striking resemblance.

It was a reincarnation.

"Ah! Goodness," continued the scholar who had not recovered from his surprise, "this is more than just unbelievable, it's crazy! It seems to me that *I am two*! I've seen you accomplish many wonders... Ah well! I believe that you've never yet attained such a degree of perfection."

"It's my true faith," acknowledged Chantecoq, contemplating himself in the mirror.

And modestly he added, "Only, my credit is much lesser than you think! In all the time I've known you, I had ample time to study you at leisure, in plain sight. And then, without you being aware, you *posed* so kindly, so complacently. Operating conditions are rarely so favourable.

"Just as, for that poor Colonel Richard, I had great difficulty creating a passable likeness for myself. Bear in mind I'd only seen him once, and for barely half an hour. It's fortunate that I was able to procure his most recent photograph. Without that I would indeed have had trouble 'capturing' my fellow. And yet… it worked as though on wheels."

More and more pleased with himself, Chantecoq, putting on the black frock coat he had prepared, added, "I've earned a medal made from chocolate!"

As Monsieur Aubry was rising to his feet, Chantecoq stopped him.

"I'm not finished. We need to talk. Not for long, but seriously, in a definitive fashion."

And straddling the back of a chair, the bloodhound continued. "You told me, didn't you, that you had a meeting this evening, at seven o'clock with Fake Richard number 2? Given that I'm Fake Richard number 1."

"Boulevard Denain, on the Terminus terrace," declared the combat aircraft's inventor.

"Good. You also recounted to me what this scoundrel asked of you before taking the train with him, to reconstitute your formula."

"That's it. I'm forced to admit that I've not yet had time."

"I'm sure you haven't. But might you be able to… cook one up for me, in five seconds. Not the real one, naturally, but something fun. When I say fun, I mean… how can I put it… I'm not a chemist, myself…"

"I guess your meaning," said Jean Aubry with a smile.
"Let's see…"

"You want a formula for an explosive which would rebound against those who used it."

"That's it, exactly."

"And which would blow up the engines into which it was loaded."

"You have indeed guessed my thoughts completely. Eh? Do you think we could play a trick against these miserables Boches?"

"It's something I've thought about for a long time," agreed the inventor. "And the fact is I've succeeded in composing an explosive such as I defy the German chemists, even after submitting it to the most scrupulous analysis, to discover the harmful element which makes it such a terrible product for those who use it. You and I can call it... fuseite. I've already talked about it to the Ministry of War who seem keenly interested in the matter."

"Very well, my friend, do you know what we're going to do?" replied Chantecoq. "You're going to give me the formula for your 'fuseite'!"

"Gladly, but I don't have it with me. I'll need to return to Saint-Mandé."

"That's quite a long way, and it's getting late."

"Do you want me to try and reconstitute it from memory?"

"How then! Because, follow me closely, if this wretch, whom I'll have the pleasure of catching red-handed, asked you to accompany him to Douai with the formula for Explosive Z, it's because he intends to steal it from you on the way.

"So, naturally, I'll let him do so, and we'll kill two birds with one stone. Not only will this spy, to whom I'll stick closer than a shadow, lead me to the whole gang of which he must be one of the most distinguished members... but we'll also slip into the hands of our enemies, entirely innocently, a terrible weapon which will backfire on them."

"That's my aim!"

"Eh! As they say in Montmartre, don't you think, my dear collaborator, it's a beauty?"

"Certainly!" agreed the scholar, "and I even consider, my dear friend, that you're the only one in the world capable of succeeding in such a formidable task."

"Very well," concluded the policeman, who seemed delighted with the turn that events had taken, "let's return to my office. You'll find everything you need to write in there."

A few seconds later, Monsieur Aubry, seated at the detective's desk, his head in his hands, completely isolated from the world, was thinking.

Standing close by, immobile, holding his breath, Chantecoq waited.

Ten minutes passed, in the most complete silence.

Then, without speaking a word, the inventor of Explosive Z picked up a pencil which was within his reach and, on a white sheet which was spread over a blotter, he wrote without hesitation a rather brief formula that he handed to his look-alike, saying simply,

"There, it's done!"

"Ah! My friend!" the bloodhound cried with the greatest joy. "What a great trick I'll be able to play, thanks to you, on those brigands! Now, I think it's time to head to the area near Gare du Nord."

"And me, what I must do?" asked Captain Evrard's father-in-law.

"I was just going to tell you," replied the policeman. "You're going to stay here until nightfall, first because it would be dangerous for us to be seen leaving together."

"Agreed."

"You'll then go home to Saint-Mandé in a closed car, taking care to avoid showing your face."

"Understood."

"I beg your pardon for bossing you about like this."

"But it's vital, dear friend, and be sure your instructions will be followed to the letter."

"I'm sure of that! But that's not all."

"Speak!"

"Tomorrow morning, you'll take the first train for Maubeuge, where I'll join you in the evening. Can I count on you, dear friend?"

"As always!"

"Thank you!"

And while taking leave of Jean Aubry, he added, "So it's agreed? Tomorrow evening at Maubeuge, for dinner."

"Under what disguise?" the inventor asked with a smile.

"I don't know yet," replied the bloodhound, "But be sure that whether I'm in my own skin or another's, which will also be my own, I'll be there to sit down to table with you."

"See you tomorrow evening, then!"

From the doorway, Chantecoq called gaily, "Warn Madame Evrard that there's every chance I'll be very hungry."

"It will be done."

"Soup and beef, an omelette and a chicken."

"Understood."

"And I," said the detective as he vanished, "I'll take care of dessert."

19 FACE TO FACE

When Chantecoq arrived outside Café Terminus, despite all the self-control he possessed, he had to acknowledge his heart was thumping a little louder than usual.

It was because he was aware he was about to play one of the most dangerous games of his life.

The adversary he had to fight, he felt was the most formidable of all.

Indeed, to have dared such a feat, he would need both audacity and extraordinary skill.

"Come on! Come on, old boy," the detective said to himself, "no nerves, or you lose three quarters of your powers. You're on the right track. If your 'client' doesn't notice the transformation, and that's certain, as brave Aubry himself was thunderstruck, you'll flip the dirty Boche as though he were in a frying pan. Yes, the road ahead is fair. Onward with confidence!

"That's it... Ah! If I wasn't haunted by the two poor ladies, who I had to leave there, both dead. It's dreadful! But the profession makes these horrible demands. In my situation I couldn't, in calling for aid which would have been useless in any case, risk being discovered and compromising everything. All the same, the unfortunates, they paid dearly for their long silence.

"But let's think no more on that. Get a grip on yourself, Chantecoq. Wipe from your mind everything which isn't the worry of the present moment, the thought of the battle that you are going to lead and that you are going to win, my old chap!

"Ah, by Jove, I think I forgot my pipe! My poor Joséphine, my best friend... No, I've got her, in the inside pocket of my frock coat. Then everything's great, I can step on to the dancefloor!"

With a tranquil and measured gait, the detective headed towards the establishment's terrace where the fake Colonel Richard, that's to say Gerfaut, or rather Colonel von Reitzer, had made his appointment with Jean Aubry.

The spy, still in the uniform of an engineering officer, was seated at a table, with a strawberry champagne before him, and was peaceably smoking a big ring cigar, a distracted, dreamy look in his eyes, as though he was far away.

"Splendid job, that man," Chantecoq acknowledged. "Aubry was right. That's completely Richard. If I hadn't handled the poor man's cadaver with my own hands, I'd swear it was really him. Oh! Let's look sharp. This time, Germany sent me an adversary of my own stature."

With an assured pace, the bloodhound approached the enemy, calling out in a voice that was a marvellous impersonation of the inventor. "Colonel, I'm not too late?"

Von Reitzer stood up, his hand held out, and said, without frowning, "Not at all, my dear Monsieur Aubry, welcome."

151

This welcome didn't contain the slightest hesitation, the smallest doubt. The German spy had been perfectly duped by the French detective.

The battle was joined, with Chantecoq holding all the cards.

Von Reitzer continued. "Sit down, then. What will you have?"

"I'm one for exemplary sobriety, even ridiculously so," the policeman declined. "I'll even offer you a confession. It's been, I'm sure, more than ten years since I've taken so much as an aperitif."

"Once isn't a habit!" the wretch insisted with that military tone of brusque cordiality. "Come now, a little quinquina[5]... a byrrh[6]?"

"Since you insist... a small quinquina."

"Waiter!"

While the spy was delivering the order to the employee, Chantecoq had a little time to cast over him one of those deep and probing glances of which he knew the secret.

Admiring as a connoisseur, as an artist, the invisible makeup with which, like himself, his companion had put to such remarkable use, he couldn't stop himself repeating under his breath, "Splendid, absolutely splendid! I only ever met one person in the world capable of rivalling me in the art of disguise. Furthermore that individual was a woman, Emma Lückner. Surely, unless I'm very much mistaken, this

---

[5] An aromatised wine, containing cinchona bark, which contains quinine - also used in treating malaria.

[6] A slightly more specific aromatised apéritif wine, byrrh contains red wine, mistelle (partially-fermented grape juice), and quinine. Marketed as a "hygiene drink", it was trademarked in the 1870s, and hugely popular through to the outbreak of the Second World War. It's still produced today, by Pernod-Ricard.

chap must be her pupil. What am I saying? Her very best pupil."

In the friendliest tone, the fake Richard continued. "You can't imagine, my dear Monsieur Aubry, how grateful I am for the favour you agreed to do for me. As the vulgar expression has it, you're getting me out of a right jam, and be assured I won't forget this."

"Only too happy to be of service," declared Chantecoq, with that tone of frank bonhomie that characterised the character whose role he was currently playing.

"This is doubtless going to inconvenience you greatly."

"Not at all. However, I admit that I wouldn't mind observing firsthand what alterations those gentlemen in the offices made to my formula, which was of luminous simplicity. I've been able to reconstitute it. It's here, in my briefcase. In that way, I'm sure you'll be able to manufacture an explosive which won't be abused by any untimely collaboration.

"Then, Colonel, we'll be doing a great service to our country. You by making me aware of your concerns, me, by frustrating the antics of those people who perhaps don't have ill intentions, but whose pride often makes them exceed the limits of imprudence and foolishness."

"Well spoken, indeed!" von Reitzer said, raising his glass in approval.

"And your daughter?" the detective asked point blank.

"She's well… thank you."

Then, wetting his lips in the glass that a server had just refilled, the fake Jean Aubry made a small grimace while saying, "Ah well, no, decidedly, these beverages don't agree with me… which however isn't to say that I disdain a fine bottle of Bordeaux, or Bourgogne…"

"Or champagne?" insinuated the Teuton, his gourmand's eye staring avidly.

"Or champagne, indeed," stressed the great bloodhound.

"So…" offered von Reitzer, "shall we go to dinner?"

"With pleasure… but on one condition, that you'll be my guest."

"Not at all! That's you!" the spy retorted sharply.

"I beg your pardon."

"There's no need, you would offend me by refusing."

"In that case, so be it!"

"Excellent, let's go in!"

The fake Colonel Richard, after tossing a silver coin to the waiter, entered the establishment's interior, followed by the fake Aubry.

Pointing to a rather isolated table, he said, "We'll be left in peace there!"

"If you want!" Chantecoq accepted.

Von Reitzer took the menu from a waiter. "What would you like?" he asked the bloodhound.

"Everything!" he replied roundly.

"Really?"

"My word of honour!"

"I beg you, don't put yourself out."

"You neither. I have an exquisitely compliant stomach, and I won't hide from you the fact that I have a truly valiant fork hand."

"Me too!"

"Decidedly, Colonel, I see that we're ever more certain to get along together."

And slowly, wisely, the spy ordered a copious menu… a little heavy… rather spicy… choosing to begin with a bottle of Graves, then retaining for the roast course a bottle of

Corton, and ordering a bottle of Mumm Cordon Rouge to cleanse their palettes.

"You want to get me sozzled, don't you," Chantecoq said to himself, "But we'll soon see which of us is best at that little game."

For form's sake, however, he protested. "Colonel, it's too much, far too much…"

"You told me," the fake Richard objected, "that you can't bear apéritifs, but that you love a bordeaux, bourgogne, or a champagne…"

"I don't deny it! But three bottles for two people! Do you want us to take the train out of our heads?"

"What a joke! Once we're installed in a decent first class compartment, we'll just take a nap until we get to Douai. Nothing better than to digest a good meal in peace. Anyway, you told me: your stomach is compliant. Come on, let's get on with it!"

"I've nothing more to say!" confessed Chantecoq, who was thinking, "I see you coming! Without knowing, you're unfolding your plan to me with the most delicious candour; but as it's in perfect accord with my own, I'll be careful not to contradict it in any way. Only I'll arrange myself in such a way that it will be the man who wants to intoxicate me who instead ends up with a sore head. Now, I've every reason to believe this will be an easy thing to manage."

Just as Chantecoq had announced, he was gifted with a very fine fork hand.

His partner, or rather his adversary, seemed to need not to give him any quarter on this terrain.

They both drank equally. Before the starters, the bottle of Graves was empty.

In a low voice, von Reitzer ordered a Haut-Barsac, and as the Corton was finished before the roast, he asked for a bottle of Pomard, in which not a single drop remained by the time the host gave the order to pop the champagne cork.

"By Jove, by Jove," said Chantecoq to himself, observing his adversary remained as calm as if he had been drinking fresh water. "He's like me, that bird, he's immune to intoxication. And I was hoping... Well, as long as he believes I'm flattened, that's the main thing!"

The detective, who knew all the slightest tricks of his trade and never neglected to employ the little strings when they seemed useful to the success of his enterprise, had taken care, gradually, and with true artistry, to adopt the face and bearing, not of a professional boozer, but a man who, dizzy from too good cheer felt rather vague in his soul and began to see trouble and to splutter, all while nevertheless keeping the tone and attitude of a man of the world whose education could only be very slightly broken down by this momentary forgetfulness of propriety.

Blinking, his mouth damp, his words slightly slurred, his gestures heavy and nonchalant, his back leaning slightly against the bench, the cunning fellow, while lighting with an uncertain hand a splendid Havana that his partner had chosen from one of the numerous boxes that encumbered the table, kept repeating, "You're really so kind! You're spoiling me... it's too much! Far too much! And I who, this morning, when you came to see me at Saint-Mandé, didn't even offer you refreshments. But the very next time you come back to see me, I'll make up for it."

And seeming a little half-softened... half-jokingly, the fake inventor threatened the Colonel with his finger, almost stuttering, "You'll pay me for this, my lad... you'll pay me!"

Von Reitzer, without revealing any of the proud satisfaction with which he was stuffed, thought, "I've got you, my lad… and now, you won't weigh heavy on my hands."

And he added, still internally, "It's extraordinary how easy to dupe these men of genius, or supposed such, often are! It's there that the colossal superiority of German *kultur* over French culture becomes apparent. No scholar in Berlin would let himself be fooled like a Paris policeman like this."

With his marvellous perspicacity, Chantecoq could well guess what was going through his companion's mind.

He was enjoying himself enormously, so much more delighted, in waiting for the definitive success of which he was now absolutely certain, that he was making a fool of a Boche, in whom he recognised, as a spy, considerable value.

So he continued, passing gradually from flashes of the most affectionate gratitude to demonstrations of the most touching tenderness. "I'm so happy to have met you, to be going there with you! Ah! We're going to do good work together! And against the Germans again! If you only knew how much I hate them, those birds! You too, right?"

"Naturally," agreed von Reitzer, who was beginning to champ at the bit.

"A French officer," continued the fake Aubry, "can only despise that race… because a French officer is honour and loyalty incarnate. But I, before you, I, Jean Aubry, the inventor of the combat aircraft, I, Jean Aubry, father of Explosive Z… I have reasons to despise them further.

"Imagine, a German officer hypocritically infiltrated my home, and got hold of my plans."

"Yes, yes," cut in the traitor, who didn't seem keen to venture on to this subject. "I know that story, as well as the

157

real drama in which Mademoiselle your daughter got herself involved... who I believe is today the wife of Captain Evrard."

"That's right. Eh? Do you think that it's not dishonouring herself to accept a role such as Lieutenant Wilhelm Ansbach played with regard to us? A German officer agreeing to become a spy, that's the sort of thing you'd only see in Germany! That's why I grant them my undying hatred... undying, you hear me, and I'll do them all the mischief I can. Because they disgust me!

"Come on, pour me a glass of liqueur, and let's drink to France's health."

"That's right! To France," agreed von Reitzer, filling the glass that his guest raised.

Slopping half of its contents on the table, Chantecoq stuttered in a voice which was more and more slurred, "And to Germany's destruction!"

This time the Colonel didn't respond.

He contented himself with clinking his glass against that of the detective.

Then, brusquely, he said, "It must be time to head to the station."

"You're right!" Chantecoq opined, "It would be too daft if we missed the train."

"Waiter! The bill," called out the fake Colonel Richard.

That formality accomplished, the two men rose from the table. "Oh!" said the bloodhound, "I can feel my legs are a bit wobbly. You entertained me too well."

"A decent nap, and it'll be nothing," repeated the spy.

"You," the policeman said to himself, "want me to sleep. Well, so be it, I'll sleep! But I'll keep one eye open. Because you don't suspect, scoundrel, the little trick I've got in store for you."

On leaving the restaurant to cross the square, Chantecoq who, without adopting a staggering walk, was however giving the highly precise impression of a man who is not at all rejoicing in the complete command of his ambulatory faculties, leaned slightly on the German's arm, while continuing to utter sayings which were beginning to sound somewhat incoherent.

When both entered the hall, the detective, whose tongue appeared to be more and more embarrassed, said, "Let's go… take… take the tickets."

"It's done," declared von Reitzer.

"No, but…"

"Don't worry about anything. Come!"

Docile, Jean Aubry allowed himself to be guided to the platform where the Douai train was sitting.

The spy officer chose a compartment in which none of the seats were occupied, helped Chantecoq to climb up, and sat opposite him.

"Would you like an evening paper?" he offered, very amiably.

"Oh yes, that would be lovely," the bloodhound accepted, adding, "Let's hope we'll be alone."

"There's every chance of that," replied the Teuton. "We only have another three minutes before the train departs, and I see no threatening silhouettes on the platform."

Chantecoq unfolded his newspaper, and pretended to read it.

But in reality, his thoughts were elsewhere.

He was thinking, "Now I'm all set. I know this rogue's plan by heart. Oh, he'll not do me any harm! He'll take advantage of my slumber to get the formula which he knows I placed in my briefcase. I'll let him do that, quite simply. His plan successful, he'll get off at the next station.

"Then I'll wake up, I'll tail him quietly, and afterwards… ah well, afterwards, that's my business.

"Good work, my old Chantecoq. It's all working out. You're as sure to win the second sleeve as the first.

"What a shame that I can't smoke a good pipe! My poor Joséphine, you're going to judge me for leaving you idle like that. But don't worry. We'll make up for it, perhaps sooner than you think!"

Already whistles were sounding. The train was about to move off… when the door, opening suddenly, made way for a lady who was already of 'a certain age' but still rather slim, and who was helped up by a compliant employee who quickly passed her a rather voluminous travel bag.

The newcomer, who was wearing an elegantly sober perfume, had her head enveloped in a veil that was insufficiently thick to hide the signs of a lupus rash, or a port wine stain that ravaged half her face.

She sat in a corner, on the other side of the compartment, immediately adopting the attitude of a person intending to isolate themselves completely and pay no attention to anything around her.

"Oh great!" Chantecoq said to himself. "She would have to come and bother us, that one! When everything was going so well…"

But, noticing that von Reitzer, on seeing the traveller, had remained impassive, he thought, "Hold on, hold on! Could there be in this bandit's plan some factor I didn't foresee? Did my flair let me down? Could it be this woman is his accomplice? Is that it? Yes, at last, I understand…

"My old Chantecoq, instead of closing your eyes, I rather think it's time to open them!"

20 THE SUDDEN ATTACK

For around an hour, the train thundered through the countryside at top speed.

Chantecoq, who had completely changed the tactic that he had at first conceived, continued to feign being absorbed in reading the newspaper that von Reitzer had passed to him.

As to that fake Colonel, after having tossed his kepi into his bag and putting on a travelling hat, he seemed to plunge into a blissful sleep inspired by pleasant digestion.

"Invitation to the waltz…" the detective said to himself. "But, very little… I'm not walking."

From time to time, he cast a furtive glance at the woman who, her head turned towards the window, appeared, in a sad and melancholy pose, to contemplate with a strange fixedness the countryside which was rolling past in the bright June night.

The policeman dearly wanted to engage in conversation with this mysterious lady, who inspired ever greater suspicion in him.

He quickly found a pretext.

"Madame," he said in a voice full of deference, "I beg your pardon for disturbing you, but don't you find it's terribly hot in here?"

"Indeed," murmured the stranger, without turning her head.

"Would it bother you if a window was opened? On my side, naturally?"

"Not at all, Monsieur."

As Chantecoq carried out the manoeuvre, the fake Colonel Richard, opening his eyes, said in a low voice, "You're letting in a bit of air, Monsieur Aubry. You're right, that can't do any harm. In fact, that light is rather irritating."

And, standing up, he went to tilt the little blue shade, designed to attenuate the glare of the luminous globe placed in the middle of the compartment when, changing his mind, he said to the woman,

"Excuse me, Madame, but I ought to ask you first if you would mind?"

"Not at all," replied the lady, still fixed in the same pose.

Now, it was almost dark.

The spy resumed his seat, and resumed his nap.

The woman seemed ever deeper in her reverie.

As to Chantecoq, who had returned to his seat, he thought, "I'd wager tuppence the party's about to start. I'll even bet four on a sudden attack. I only have to see it coming, and need to let it happen, without of course neglecting the crucial precautions in such cases…"

And, very slowly, the detective, slipping his hand into the inside pocket of his frock coat, immediately encountered the butt of a Browning, the latest model, which was Joséphine's peaceful neighbour.

It was time.

Hardly had he made that gesture when, rousing himself suddenly from the sleep which he had been pretending to resume, von Reitzer stood up, bursting into movement as though powered by a spring, and threw himself at the throat of the fake Jean Aubry who thought at once:

"There we are, the sudden attack. The woman is… Chantecoq, save your skin, old chap!"

And unleashing a violent punch, a left jab, into his adversary's stomach, he sent him bouncing from the cushions, all while retaining his admirable sang-froid and shouting out,

"Ah! Colonel Richard, have you gone mad?"

But von Reitzer, who also seemed gifted with Herculean strength, stood up at once, and threw himself again on his adversary, with unheard of violence. Chantecoq, understanding that things were escalating and they wanted, not only the contents of his briefcase, but also his very life, had wrapped his hand around his revolver, whose butt was pressed against the spy's chest.

Chantecoq didn't have time to pull the trigger.

A pain as acute as it was sudden had made him stagger.

It was the traveller who, profiting from the few seconds of astonishment into which the spy's brutal aggression had thrown Chantecoq, had slipped behind him like a grass snake, half-stunning him with a violent blow from the knuckle-dusters that she was holding tight between her fingers and with which she had thumped him on the neck.

The detective didn't fall right away.

His vitality was so great, his energy was so potent, his will to triumph so sublime, that he tried to keep fighting, trying to encircle his adversary's bullish neck with his steely fingers.

But a first attack of dizziness convinced him to give up attacking the enemy head-on.

"The cowards," he thought, "but it's not over. They're stronger, I must be the most cunning."

And he let himself fall full-length on to the bench, as though senseless, stiffening with the sublime effort of not losing consciousness, of staying awake, to see what they would do.

Oh! It didn't take long.

Von Reitzer rushed to put his foot over the Browning that Chantecoq had dropped and which had fallen to the floor.

And just as, several days beforehand, he had thrown himself on Colonel Richard, murdered by his accomplices, to steal his secret, he rushed feverishly towards he whom he still mistook for Jean Aubry and, unbuttoning his frock coat, he rummaged in the pocket, grabbed the wallet, and while the mysterious woman was opening the lampshade, flooding the compartment with sudden light, he searched through the scholar's papers for the precious document.

Chantecoq was watching him through half-closed eyelids.

"Go on… brigand! Go on, rogue!" he thought. "It doesn't matter if I pay for this adventure with my life. Thanks to me, without them suspecting it for a moment, our enemies will bring home the very cause of their own future defeat."

And as he felt himself weakening, he thought, "All the same, I'd prefer not to die! Because I still have duties to fulfil. And then… and then, how to warn the others? Come now, no weakness! Something tells me the wound isn't fatal. I've had worse… And I also believe the best way for me to live, is to appear to be utterly dead."

And he remained immobile, inert, with the appearance of already being a corpse.

Von Reitzer was continuing his examination of the papers.

"Well then, you can't find it?"

"Yes, yes, here it is."

"You're sure it's that one?"

"Absolutely sure."

"In that case, it only remains for us to get off the train."

"Karl von Talberg ought to be waiting for us in a car."

"Karl von Talberg," Chantecoq noted heroically. "He's there too! Ah, very good. I'll end up having the whole list."

As for the spy, he was asking a question in German, a language with which however our detective was as familiar as with his own.

"What are we going to do with Aubry?"

"What if we threw him out the door?"

"Let's leave him there."

"Indeed, that would perhaps be better, because of the train stopping."

On hearing those words, despite his indomitable energy, Chantecoq shuddered to the core of his being.

"No! No!" he rebelled. "They won't get me like that."

And reaching for his revolver which, free from the pressure von Reitzer had been placing on it, was now within reach of his hand, Chantecoq was about to grab hold of it when a cry rang out.

"Watch out!"

It was the woman who, not having stopped watching the victim, foresaw his saving action.

Like a savage, the fake Richard thrust a knee into Chantecoq's chest, pressing down with his full weight.

In a hoarse voice, he cried out, "I've got him! Open the door, open it quickly!"

But the veiled woman wasn't moving.

She was staring with rapt attention at an object she had just picked up from the bench.

That object was... Joséphine, the policeman's pipe, which he, quite unaware, had knocked from his pocket while grabbing his revolver.

"Open it, then..." von Reitzer insisted.

"Not yet!" replied the mysterious woman.

And showing the pipe to the spy, she added, "Do you see that?"

"Yes, what of it?"

"What of it... well... nothing. But it just revealed something extraordinary to me. We have succeeded better than I could ever have hoped.

"The man you're holding, he's not Jean Aubry, inventor of Explosive Z. It's the detective Chantecoq, our deadliest enemy!

"His pipe, that I know so well, his Joséphine, his best friend, just betrayed him. This time, he's ours, he won't escape us."

"Emma Lückner!" roared the detective who tried, vainly, to free himself.

"Yes, Emma Lückner," hissed Wilhelm's spy. "Emma Lückner, emerged alive from the tomb in which you thought her so safely buried forever. Emma Lückner resuscitated, not only to finish her work that you interrupted, but to be avenged on you!"

"Wretch! Pig!" the intrepid bloodhound called out.

But a purple cloud was blossoming before his eyes.

Feeling life abandoning him, he gave a jolt, one last effort, a rattle, and fell back stiff, inanimate.

"Dead!" said von Reitzer.

"No, passed out, alive. Just how I wanted to take him," hissed the viper.

And Wilhelm's spy, whose eyes glittered with the most criminal glee, tore off the mask of flimsy fabric that covered her face and, blazing with the most diabolical beauty, she cried, shivering with the most dreadful passion that could stir the vilest of women, "Mikaël, my lips are yours."

Like a madman, Colonel von Reitzer rushed into the arms that were wide open for him, while Emma Lückner murmured, crushed beneath his brutal kiss:

"Now, France is ours!"

21 JEAN AUBRY'S WORRIES

Just like every other day, Lieutenant Vallier was working in his office, with unparalleled dedication; because since the disappearance of Colonel Richard, of whom he was the assiduous colleague, all technical and administrative duties had devolved to him.

The only one up to date with his boss on a great number of details that the interests of national security forbade him from confiding in a third person, he alone had to take on this whole enormous labour.

However, he acquitted himself marvellously.

Gifted with rare intelligence, capable of the most formidable efforts, he had been in no way crushed by these responsibilities.

Quite the contrary, he had demonstrated a perfect method, at the same time as an incomparable work ethic, stimulated both by his duty and by his love for the charming Yvonne.

But time was passing, and still no news of Colonel Richard, or Monsieur Dalibert, who, however, had promised a favourable response in less than forty-eight hours.

He really needed to make a decision.

The newspaper article that Marois had cruelly shown the orphan didn't permit the slightest hesitation, the slightest reticence.

It was vital to cut short the outrageous hypotheses engendered by the Colonel's mysterious departure and his entourage's silence.

It was crucial to act without delay.

Mademoiselle Richard and Lieutenant Vallier, after consulting, at once agreed that the moment to intervene had come.

Following those steps, General Framer, who commanded the region, a first class militarist, doubled with the most remarkable moral qualities, put himself in touch at once with Douai's public prosecutor.

All of them, concerned by the unexpected incident, and sensing foul play, after secretly warning their respective bosses, made mutual promises to work hand in hand, indissolubly united.

The prosecutor would communicate the full results produced by the inquiry that he was going to order at once.

The General would furnish the prosecutor with all the necessary information.

Nearly a week passed without the inquiry having taken a single step.

Despite the police's discretion, the case had however leaked to the public.

In the area, the most extraordinary rumours were starting to be peddled, and the day before, a great Parisian daily paper had published a sensational article, recounting that the disappearance of Colonel Richard, director of Douai's powder mill, was now a proven fact, and that without being able to establish the crime's motive as yet, it was obvious that the unfortunate commanding officer had been murdered.

Faced with this dreadful reality, Mademoiselle Richard had lost all hope.

Although the Lieutenant had the conviction, the certainty of having seen his boss again, of having spoken to him, of having heard from his lips the formal order to hold his tongue, he no longer dared to shine, in the eyes of she whom he loved, a confidence in a return which was becoming more and more problematic for him.

He was about to quit his desk to report to inspect one of the workshops; because, despite the formidable labour by which he was crushed, he wasn't neglecting his usual surveillance of the workers, when the orderly came to warn him that a gentleman wished to speak to him.

The gentleman was none other than Jean Aubry.

He, after having travelled to Maubeuge, had waited in vain for the detective.

The inventor wasn't too worried about missing him at the rendez-vous.

He told himself, "He's now embarked on a case which is so serious that there's nothing astonishing, after all, in him being obliged to modify his schedule. However, I'm surprised that he, who's always so punctual, didn't send us a telegram or a letter.

"In the end, we shall see. The main thing is that nothing untoward has happened to him. On that score, I'm not worried. He's crafty enough to pass through all dangers and

171

through all traps. It's not for nothing that those who know him call him 'the elusive one'.'"

The following day, Monsieur Aubry, who, due to his works in progress, couldn't stay away from his laboratory for long, had returned to Saint-Mandé, assuming that he would soon receive news of his friend Chantecoq.

But time passed, and the bloodhound still didn't provide him with any signs of life.

Aubry began to worry.

First he went to Avenue Trudaine, where the policeman lived under the name of Monsieur Chavard.

The concierge told him his lodger had already been travelling for over a week, and that she had no idea when he would return, adding, clearly hostile and malevolent, "He's such a funny sort. With him you never know on what foot to dance. My opinion is he's a bit barmy."

The inventor hadn't pressed the matter. He had gone straight away to Sûreté générale, had asked to be received by the director, Monsieur Servières, who knowing the great scholar and professing the keenest admiration for him, had ordered him to be shown directly into his office.

Without revealing to that senior civil servant the slightest portion of the grave secrets that the detective had confided in him, Monsieur Aubry didn't however hide from him that having made an appointment with Chantecoq several days earlier, he had at first been slightly surprised to see him miss it; then, in the face of his friend's silence, astonishment had changed to disquiet, which he had decided to report to the policeman's direct boss.

Monsieur Servières tried to reassure him.

"As you're brave Chantecoq's friend," he declared, "you must know him well and, as a result, you must be aware that he sometimes disappears for weeks at a time, without anyone knowing where he's gone. We let him do it. He's supple, cunning, and he has such great need of independence, that we're careful not to bother him in any way. He is, you know, our best bloodhound; and for my part, considering him superior to me, I give him completely free rein."

"Director," Jean Aubry said as he stood up, "it only remains for me to thank you a thousand times for your kindness."

"Only too happy to be of service to the genius inventor of the combat aircraft."

Germaine's father bowed.

Monsieur Servières continued. "On that subject, have you heard the news?"

"What news, Monsieur Director?"

"Of Colonel Richard's disappearance."

"Indeed, I had heard talk of it," responded the scholar evasively. Bound to Chantecoq by the most sacred oath, he would not have wanted for one moment to allow his companion to understand that he was better informed than anyone over that mysterious business.

"That must interest you," continued Monsieur Servières. "Because wasn't it to the Douai powder mill that the manufacture of your explosive was entrusted?"

"Quite so, Monsieur Director!"

"Peculiar coincidence," replied the civil servant. "As it happens, we don't have any precise news. The Douai authorities seem rather embarrassed and the silence from Chantecoq, who's certainly in the field, leads me to think that we're facing the most difficult and complicated case."

As Jean Aubry remained silent, the director of Sûreté générale took a newspaper from his desk and said, passing it to the inventor, "Here, there's that great daily paper which insinuates that this officer might have been murdered. This article's author knows nothing more about it than us, of course, although, sometimes, those journalistic gentlemen manage, I acknowledge, to show themselves as better than my best bloodhounds. I'm not speaking of Chantecoq there, of course. But for me, who knows only the bare details of this case, I wouldn't be far from admitting that this hypothesis is quite close to the truth."

While Monsieur Servières spoke, Jean Aubry skimmed through the article in question.

He was determined.

He knew.

But pledged to absolute silence until Chantecoq released him from his word, he contented himself with returning the newspaper to Monsieur Servières, saying, "It's certainly possible, that's for sure!"

The director of Sûreté générale continued. "Do you know, my dear Monsieur Aubry, the idea which has come to me?"

"No… Monsieur Director."

"Ah well! I fear the great German spy, having learned that Colonel Richard was in possession of the formula for your new explosive, murdered that poor man so as to get hold of it."

"They're indeed capable of it," declared the inventor.

"Do you think they may have succeeded in getting hold of your invention? That would be dreadful."

Then without failing his commitment, Monsieur Aubry felt he had the right to reply. "Rest easy on that subject, Monsieur. I authorise you, if you consider it useful, to repeat to the Minister of War what I'm about to say. Having already failed to be the victim of those wretches and having paid for my trusting nature with my own daughter's liberty, I've become uncommonly prudent.

"I can assure you of one thing, and that's on the faith of the oath, it's that while admitting that our enemies may have murdered Colonel Richard, I defy them to get their hands on my formula."

"Ah! I can breathe!" said the senior civil servant, who appeared to be relieved of a terrible burden.

And he added, shaking the inventor's hand, "Then, those wretches answered for their crime?"

"You said it, Monsieur Director."

He burned with the desire to question Jean Aubry further.

But the inventor, judging that he had spoken quite enough, took his leave of Monsieur Servières who didn't dare to ask any more questions of the illustrious scholar whose firm, measured and solemn words had been enough to convince him.

On leaving the offices on Rue des Saussaies, still in the grip of considerable anguish, the inventor of the combat aircraft returned home.

Increasingly anxious, the scholar spent a large portion of the night reflecting.

His friend's silence, the rumours about the Colonel's assassination, that whole atmosphere of drama, mystery and death, with which he felt himself surrounded, far from derailing his thoughts, permitted him instead to be more resolved.

"Tomorrow morning," he said, "I'll take the first train to Douai. I'll go straight to the powder mill. With all the discretion and prudence that circumstances dictate, I'll begin my own investigation.

"If Chantecoq's hiding there, he'll see me and won't hesitate to make himself known to me. In the other eventuality, then my fears will have been well-founded. And then, once certain that he too has disappeared, I will notify…"

And that's why Jean Aubry found himself, at two o'clock in the afternoon, in Lieutenant Vallier's office.

22 A THEATRICAL EFFECT

At once the ice had been broken between the two men.

Indeed, hardly had Monsieur Aubry made himself known when the young officer, who was seeing him for the first time, was bowing to him with every sign of the most respectful deference.

"My dear master," he had declared, "trust that I'm endlessly flattered to find myself in your presence. I am, indeed, one of your most enthusiastic admirers. I know how much my country owes to your genius, and permit me to assure you of my absolute devotion."

"I thank you," replied Monsieur Aubry, sitting on the armchair that the Lieutenant offered him. "I'm doubtless going to need the devotion you offer me so spontaneously."

"You see that I'm happy and proud at the prospect, my dear master."

"I know you, without you suspecting a thing," continued the inventor, very favourably impressed by Raymond Vallier's welcome. "I've heard good things about you… a lot of good things, Lieutenant, and I believe, as of now, that I can observe that they were not exaggerations."

Raymond Vallier saluted him with a charming modesty.

As, in a gesture full of delicate deference, he remained on his feet before Jean Aubry, the inventor said to him, "Please, Lieutenant, sit down. We need to have a very serious talk."

The artillery officer took his place at his desk, preparing to listen with a kind of religious fervour to the words spoken by the man whom he considered, rightly, to be a master of modern science and one of the most precious, perhaps the most useful, of our national defence auxiliaries.

Jean Aubry, who was completely lucid, replied. "You're certainly aware of my association with Colonel Richard?"

"Certainly, my dear master."

"You'll therefore be aware that it's here that my new explosive ought to be manufactured."

"Explosive Z…"

"That's the one! You must therefore understand, my dear Lieutenant, what emotion has been caused in me by the disappearance of Colonel Richard, a disappearance which has been noted officially today, and even announced by the press."

"I understand it all the better," replied Vallier, "as Colonel Richard held your formula, and I'll add, if you allow me…"

"Please, go on."

"I'll add that it's been impossible for me to get my hands on that formula which the Colonel himself deposited in his safe before my very eyes."

"Be assured," affirmed Aubry, "I have every reason to believe that the formula is secure."

And without insisting further on this subject which risked going on too long, the inventor, more determined than ever to keep the word he had given to Chantecoq, changed the subject. "I have need of other information."

"Believe me, dear master, I would be only too happy to give it to you, if possible."

"Oh! It's really very simple. Did you receive a visit from Monsieur Dalibert, an engineer for the state?"

"Indeed," Yvonne's fiancé replied. "Monsieur Dalibert twice visited the powder mill."

"When was that?" the inventor asked keenly.

"The first time…" the young officer said pointedly, "was the same day as the explosion at the artillery park."

"Very good…"

"The second was the following day, with the Colonel, who had arranged a meeting with him in his office."

"And since then?"

"Nothing more."

"That's peculiar."

"And yet, my dear master, this Monsieur Dalibert who, may I say, struck me as an extremely respectable man, also appeared very concerned that the Colonel hadn't returned since the evening before, and he promised me, as well as Mademoiselle Richard, whose disquiet seemed to move him deeply, to busy himself with tracking down our director, and to send us news within forty-eight hours, as precise as possible."

"And you've received nothing?"

"Absolutely nothing, dear master."

At this response, so categorical, Jean Aubry felt his heart clench.

For him, now, there was no doubt about it.

For Chantecoq not to have kept the promise that he had made, especially with that young girl in tears, for him to have given no sign of life to anyone, it must be that he found himself in a situation which deprived him of all resources.

And that situation, the scholar didn't dare imagine.

"I'll add," continued the Lieutenant, struck by the disquiet which he read in his visitor's face, "I'll add that Monsieur Dalibert, whose good faith we have no reason to suspect since, just the day before, the Colonel told me he would introduce me to him, asked us, Mademoiselle Yvonne and I, to maintain, until further notice, silence regarding Monsieur Richard's disappearance."

But Jean Aubry was no longer listening to the officer.

Very pale, prey to a painful anxiety, his eyes burning with deaf rage, the inventor was thinking, "So long as he wasn't also murdered!"

There was a gentle knock on the door.

Lieutenant Vallier went to open it.

It was the Colonel's daughter.

On seeing her, Raymond's face lit up, with a glow of boundless tenderness.

"Come in, Mademoiselle," he said at once with affectionate haste.

"I beg your pardon," declared Yvonne in a low voice, hovering on the threshold. "Just now, I was at my window. I saw a man cross the courtyard and enter your office. I thought I recognised, from his picture in the papers, Monsieur Jean Aubry, the famous inventor with whom my father was in correspondence…"

Choked with emotion, stopping between each word, the adorable creature managed to finish, "So, I came to see… if there was any… news… of my poor father!"

"Come in then, Mademoiselle!" Lieutenant Vallier invited her in.

180

And turning towards the scholar, he introduced her. "Mademoiselle Richard!"

"Oh! Yes, come in!" said Germaine's father, regarding the orphan with a kind and paternal air. She replied at once.

"Forgive my curiosity, but I was anxious to know. I can't cope, especially since that article in the newspaper. I tried to tell myself it's not true, it's not possible that my father is no more, that he'll surely return. I know very well that any hope is so fragile that I no longer dare to rely on it."

"Mademoiselle," replied Jean Aubry, deeply moved, because before such exquisite youth and charm beautified further by sorrow, he felt just as disarmed as if he had been facing his own daughter. "Mademoiselle, although I have the honour of meeting you for the first time, believe that my deepest, most ardent sympathy goes out to you at these cruel times."

In speaking like this, the excellent man wondered if he had the right to leave this unfortunate girl in an illusion which, by being prolonged, would make the reality still more atrocious. But then there was another knock at the door.

"Who's coming to disturb us now?" cried Raymond Vallier.

Because, from Jean Aubry's attitude, he guessed the painful but necessary resolution the man had just taken. And he went to the door, ready to dismiss the indiscreet visitor at once.

But a messenger was there, calling out, "A letter for you, Lieutenant."

"Give it here!" replied the young officer as he closed the door sharply.

On the envelope, the following heading was printed:

DOUAI FLOOR
From the office of the district attorney

"Do you mind?" asked Raymond.
Mademoiselle Richard and the inventor both nodded.
Nervously, Yvonne's fiancé unsealed the official letter.
It was composed thus:

To Monsieur Lieutenant Vallier
% the Douai (North) Powder Mill
Monsieur,

I have the sad honour and painful duty to inform you that following an anonymous report, delivered yesterday evening to my office, we went this morning to the place known as Chapelle Saint-Nicolas, and that, conforming with details contained in that letter, we discovered, hidden beneath a flagstone, the body of Colonel Richard, whose death seems to have occurred several days previously.

I entreat you to come immediately and join me at the chapel, so that we may, in your presence, proceed with the official identification of the deceased, before transporting him to Douai, for an autopsy.

Please accept, monsieur, my most sincere regards.
DEVAUX
District attorney.

Lieutenant Vallier was silent for a moment, immobile, struck in the heart by the news which had been delivered so coldly, so administratively, which would put an end to the last hope, slight as it was, which still lingered in the soul of the woman he loved.

Not daring to deliver her with the fatal blow directly, with a small, serious gesture, the young officer passed the official missive to Monsieur Aubry, who took it and read it at once.

Then the two mens' gazes met.

Yvonne spotted that glance.

She understood.

She let out a terrible cry.

"It's over!"

"Courage," said the inventor firmly.

"Courage!" repeated Raymond Vallier with a sob.

"My father! My poor father!" the poor heartbroken orphan repeated, haggard, dazed, with no tears yet.

She didn't falter, the poor girl.

Triumphing over the dreadful news which was torturing her, she instead remained… superb, valiant, rising to the challenge.

And, addressing her fiancé, she said to him, in a voice which was no longer trembling and with a hint of admirable willpower, "I want to know everything, right now, the full truth."

The officer was about to respond.

But Jean Aubry intervened. "Lieutenant," he said, "you know where your duty calls you… leave! I shall speak to Mademoiselle Yvonne."

And, overwhelmed, distraught, Vallier added, betraying himself, "I entrust her to you!"

Yvonne held out her arms to the young man who, before leaving, looked at her with eyes full of tears.

And as they both, trying to gather themselves, remained mute and bowed their heads under the weight of their sorrow, Jean Aubry, who had guessed everything, took Yvonne's hand and put it in Raymond's, saying, "Kiss, my children… I've guessed your secret!"

23 THE CADAVER

On leaving Monsieur Aubry, Raymond Vallier, overwhelmed by the news he had just learned, crossed the courtyard at a rapid pace, when he found himself facing Gerfaut, who was attentively watching the development work on pavilion B.

Without hesitation, because he had unlimited confidence in that man, who was rightly known as the best civilian worker in the powder mill, he waved him over.

Gerfaut hastened to run over, asking, "How can I be of service, Lieutenant?"

"Are you feeling better?" Vallier asked first.

"Oh yes, Lieutenant. It wasn't a big deal. I get them, these bad fevers, they knock me out, suddenly, and there's nothing to be done about it."

"Well, you're on your feet again, that's the main thing."

"Thank you, Lieutenant, and I hope it won't come over me again any time soon."

Then in a voice full of gentle deference, he added, "It's you, Lieutenant, who are in poor health. You overwork yourself, too. This would be a bad time to fall ill."

"My friend," replied Vallier, "there are exceptionally serious things going on here. I know how devoted you are to us…"

"Oh! Yes, Lieutenant."

"Since I've been here, better than anyone, I've been able to appreciate the value of your service."

"I've always done what I can, Lieutenant."

"That's why I'm not hesitating to ask you today to do me a big favour."

"With pleasure, Lieutenant."

"Colonel Richard…"

Vallier stopped, because a sob had just torn itself from his chest.

The wretch with an air of good faith which was almost candid, shouted at once, "He's returned?"

"Alas! No, my brave Gerfaut… Colonel Richard is dead."

"Ah! My God!"

"And murdered!"

"Is that possible!" the criminal cried in a voice filled with indignation and even perfectly disguised anger.

Yvonne's fiancé explained in a broken voice. "The district attorney just informed me that his body has been found in the Chapelle Saint-Nicolas."

"In the Chapelle Saint-Nicolas!" And, feigning ignorance, he added, "Chapelle Saint-Nicolas, where is that again?"

"You know very well, let's see… on the Lille road. The old sanctuary in open countryside…"

"Oh! Yes, I've got you now, Lieutenant. Forgive me, when I've had one of these fevers, I lose my memory a bit. And you're telling me our poor Colonel was found there… dead… murdered?"

"Yes, Gerfaut."

"What a tragedy! Such a brave man, and so capable with it!"

"You said it, my friend. I know how attached you were to him. So, I've come to ask you to come with me to identify him."

"Certainly, Lieutenant. Oh! Poor Colonel Richard! Who could have committed such a crime? He who was so good? He who didn't have a single enemy in the world."

"Keep your voice down, Gerfaut," suggested the officer, pointing out a group of workers who were crossing the courtyard. "We must keep this dreadful news quiet for now, because of Mademoiselle Yvonne."

"Oh! The poor child!" Gerfaut lamented hypocritically, "she will be devastated, loving her father as she did."

Almost running, the two men, who seemed equally overwhelmed, left the powder mill by a small gate which led to the countryside, and that was so as to avoid indiscreet glances and awakening premature curiosity.

They soon arrived at the old ruined sanctuary which was already surrounded by a crowd of peasants and children, kept at a respectful distance by the police.

The district attorney stood under the porch, flanked by a prosecutor, a clerk, and the police commissioner.

On noticing the artillery officer, the attorney went to him, asking, "Lieutenant Vallier, isn't it?"

"Yes, Monsieur."

"Who is this man accompanying you?"

"Our best worker, Monsieur Gerfaut, whose intelligent and diligent devotion Colonel Richard particularly appreciated."

"Come in!" the magistrate ordered them curtly. Haughty, severe, he seemed to have as high an opinion of his function as of his own person.

The officer and the murderer entered the chapel.

The Colonel's body, stripped almost bare, was lying on the altar.

Near him stood a man dressed in black, the doctor who was about to begin the first legal formalities.

Vallier, more and more overwhelmed, approached.

Then, he took a step back again.

The body, indeed, already bore signs of rather advanced decomposition.

But, mastering the painful feeling that he felt in the presence of the disfigured remains of this leader alongside whom he had lived and worked for so long, he advanced, murmuring in a choked voice, "It's really him!"

"Our poor Colonel!" Von Reitzer echoed shamelessly. In the presence of his victim, he hadn't felt the slightest shudder, the least revulsion, the smallest scrap of remorse.

Then Vallier asked, trembling with dread, pale with rage, shuddering with horror, "He really was murdered, wasn't he?"

"By Jove!" the district attorney said rather drily.

And, pointing to the man dressed in black who had not left the altar, he added, still distant and full of solemn importance, "Doctor Saint-Pol has already discovered, behind the neck, the trace of a bullet which must have passed through the cranium and caused instant death. The autopsy will establish the time of death and the circumstances in which it occurred."

At once, the prosecutor, a rather young man who seemed very anxious to get down to action, added, with an excessive volubility which denoted an essentially impulsive character and a slight accent which revealed he was originally from Marseille: "What a strange business! Was this unfortunate officer led into an ambush so as to rob him?

"At first glance, the fact that we found him devoid of his clothes could lead one to think that theft was the motive behind the crime. But, thinking about it, given that Colonel Richard must only have had a very small amount of money on him, I come to wonder, *a priori*, simply *a priori*, gentlemen, if this staging might not have been set up cleverly by the guilty party, so as to allay initial suspicions.

"Also, the more I think about it, the more I think that this unfortunate man must have been the victim of some mysterious and personal vendetta."

"And yet…" the Lieutenant felt he had to interrupt. "Our Colonel had nothing but friends."

"It's possible…" replied the prosecutor. "But he could also have had ladyfriends."

"What do you mean to insinuate by that, monsieur?" Yvonee's fiancé shouted.

"It's very simple," retorted the young magistrate. "Colonel Richard was a widow, wasn't he?"

"Yes, Monsieur."

"Well, he wasn't yet of an age where one renounces the joys of love."

"Monsieur…"

"He must certainly have had a mistress."

"Monsieur prosecutor…"

"Or two!"

"Permit me…"

"And it's on that side of things that I'm going to focus my first enquiries. Because everything so far leads me to think that this is all mixed up in a tragic love story."

This time, Vallier burst out. "Monsieur, I can't allow you to so injure the memory of a man whose private life must be, for you as for everybody, free of all blemishes."

"What do you know about it?" the prosecutor retorted bitterly, becoming decidedly aggressive.

Vallier was about to reply, but the attorney intervened. "Monsieur Faraud de la Rescasse, this is not the moment to carry out interrogations, especially in the presence of this body. Now the corpse has been identified, it only remains to transport it to Douai."

"Monsieur," said the officer, "may I ask you when the Colonel's mortal remains will be released to Mademoiselle Richard?"

"As soon as the autopsy has been carried out, I'll let you know."

Vallier bowed.

The magistrates left, while some community-minded peasants took hold of the body and, after having wrapped it in a sheet, carried it on a stretcher over to a covered sleigh that had been brought to the chapel by the small path.

Then, bare-headed, Vallier and Gerfaut followed the vehicle which headed towards town.

"Well! Lieutenant," murmured Gerfaut. "What do you make of that?"

"I don't know any more," replied the officer. "I wonder... I think... I don't know... I find nothing... nothing..."

"Ah well!" said the wretch, in a low voice, "do you want my advice?"

"Speak, Gerfaut."

And casting a strange look at Vallier, von Reitzer, the spy, the traitor, the murderer, dared to insinuate, "If you ask me, you see, the murderer isn't far away. And I'd bet my fortnight that justice won't take long to find him!"

24 THE ARREST

Broken by pain, almost fainting beneath her long black veils, Yvonne Richard, supported by Jean Aubry, walked towards the gaping hole where her father's coffin had just descended for ever.

An old priest, in a compassionate gesture, held out the silver aspergillum to her.

Calling on all her courage, the orphan sketched a vague sign of the cross while murmuring, in a heartbreaking sob, "Adieu, my dear papa, adieu!"

Then, broken, she fell back into the inventor's arms.

General Framer, commanding the military contingent, stepped forward then, followed by a delegation of officers in dress uniform and uttered these words in a vibrant voice which resonated throughout the cemetery, over which a tragic silence had fallen.

"Adieu, Colonel Richard! Adieu, our brother in arms! You fell victim to the most odious of crimes.

"But we will avenge your memory, I swear to you, in the name of the friendship which united us, in the name of all those who never ceased to love you and to respect you, one of the French army's most brilliant officers!"

While the ranks parted to let through Jean Aubry who was leading Yvonne, shattered by grief, then the General who, at a smart pace, and followed by his staff, reached the cemetery gate, Raymond Vallier, prey to an emotion which was expressed not with tears, but with a touching pallor, grasped with an almost hesitant hand the aspergillum that a choirboy passed to him.

Then, all around, murmurs rumbled, not, this time, sympathetic and sorrowful, but harsh, prolonged, aggressive… and where one detected a menacing indignation that only the sanctity of the place and the solemn ceremony which was unfolding prevented from escalating.

Vallier, nevertheless, was about to bless the coffin, when a strong hand grasped his arm,and a voice hissed in his ears.

"No, not you! I forbid you!"

"Gerfaut, you're mad," cried Yvonne's fiancé, staring into the face of the worker who was casting a gaze full of defiance at him.

"Murderer!" the nightwatchman said simply, between gritted teeth.

Then he tore the aspergillum from the officer brusquely, to the approval of several cries that were still moderate, but already clearer.

"He's right!"

A rumour built suddenly, like the distant roar of a sea which was beginning to raise a storm. "Murderer! Murderer!"

Proudly, Vallier raised his head, staring bravely at all those surrounding him.

No words escaped his lips. But everything in him seemed to protest: "What! It's me whom you dare to accuse? Me? Me!"

And he remained immobile, his head high, his eyes clear, his nostrils flaring, defying those who were insulting him so more eloquently than he could have done with any words.

The clamour echoed.

Now the cries, "Murderer! Murderer!" were ringing violently from robust chests, climbing into the air, powerful and prolonged.

Fists were clenched.

Some of the women hid their faces, others crossed themselves, scandalised, alarmed.

Was a dreadful, unexpected drama about to play out around this open tomb?

General Framer, a superb man, with a proud gait, and a face imprinted with masculine resolution, retraced his steps, surprised by these grumbles and cries.

In his resonant voice, he shouted, "Who dares accuse a French officer of being a murderer?"

At those words, silence fell as if by magic.

Gerfaut had vanished into the crowd, which instantly became calm, respectful, assuaged.

Then, addressing Raymond Vallier, who remained in an attitude full of restrained bravado, General Framer said simply, "Come, Lieutenant. Don't respond to these imbeciles. Your dignity defends you, as does the sanctity of this place that no one has any right to disturb. Come!"

The artillery officer, still calm and with his head held high, followed his commanding officer who, once beyond the cemetery, drew him close to talk to him.

193

"You're aware of the rumours that have been circulating on your account?"

"Yes, General," Yvonne's fiancé replied firmly. "I know that I'm accused of being Colonel Richard's assassin. Up to now I had treated this calumny with contempt, circulated doubtless by the true guilty parties who have an interest in deflecting police suspicions."

"That's absolutely my opinion," intoned the General, "and be sure, Lieutenant, that I'm ready to cover you with my trust and my esteem. That, for the moment, must be sufficient for you!"

"Thank you, General," Vallier replied. "But if up to now I repulsed this odious accusation with contempt, which in any case was only due to insinuations as cowardly as they were anonymous, today it was defined in a way that was so startling, I have the honour to place a charge of defamation against the worker Gerfaut who, at least, had the courage to speak to me out loud, voicing the dreadful insult that many unthinking people were already murmuring."

"Your request, my dear Lieutenant," replied the General, "is far too fair for me not to follow it up immediately. On our return to town, I'll transmit it straight away to the civil authorities with the most favourable opinions. Count on me to defend to the hilt the honour of an officer whom I respect and love."

"General, thank you again."

"Your hand, my friend…"

Before the crowd which was moving forwards, the noble leader clasped the young Lieutenant's hand vigorously, saying to him, so as to be heard by all those who had approached and were silently observing this scene:

"I won't tell you to be brave! You have bravery to spare! I really hope, however, that within twenty-four hours, your slanderers will return to the shadows which befit vipers and cowards!"

Reassured by this demonstration which gave him all necessary authority to keep his head through the storm, Raymond Vallier left rapidly, his head high, ready to riposte all attacks.

While crossing the twelve hundred metres which separated the cemetery from the powder mill, the young officer was lost in thought.

"Who could have put into circulation this infernal rumour which runs since the discovery of my poor Colonel's corpse? On what grounds could they accuse me of such an abominable crime?

"How is that it was Gerfaut who uttered this terrible accusation to my face? Gerfaut, our best worker. Gerfaut, a serious, reflective man, considered above all, who would never give himself over, in the middle of a cemetery, and in such painful circumstances to such a scandalous rant, if he didn't have reason to believe that he was speaking the truth?"

Faced with the impossibility of answering those questions, Yvonne's fiancé thought: "It's all very troubling and I see only a sombre machination conducted against me by the true guilty parties.

"The wretches! So long as my poor dear mother hasn't had wind of this outrageous calumny. Oh! I know she knows me too well to lend credence, even for a moment, to such ideas. But the idea that I'm the butt of these outrages by scoundrels and imbeciles would be enough to overwhelm her. She is so frail... so exhausted by age.

"Presently, I'll take my bicycle and I'll go to Saint-Vincent to visit her… and, if necessary, prove to her that, with a clear conscience and with the support of my superiors, my honour has nothing to fear from these contemptible slurs."

Saint-Vincent was a retirement home run by nuns where, in view of the incessant care that she demanded, Raymond Vallier had admitted his mother, whom he cherished with all the tenderness of his heart which was deeply generous and filial.

"Poor mother!" he murmured with emotion, "who is so proud of her son and who so hopes, before she dies, to see me become a Captain and Chevalier of the Legion of Honour!

"Her dream will come true. All this, I'm sure, is only a bad patch, which will doubtless be dissipated."

However, when he entered the powder mill, heading towards the cottage where Mademoiselle Richard had returned directly after the ceremony with Monsieur Aubry who, a friend since just the day before, but as devoted as if he had been so for the last twenty years, had not left the orphan's side, the young officer felt overcome by a shadow of unspeakable sadness, composed of heavy anguish and vague presentiment.

It was with a dry throat that he rang at the door which opened almost immediately, revealing the elderly Françoise who, still tearful, couldn't repress a flinch of dread on seeing the officer.

Raymond, stepping forward, reproached her very quietly. "So, you also believe I'm to blame?"

Overwhelmed, the servant, not daring to refuse access to the building to the man who, in her naive credulity, she believed, because she had been told so, to be her master's murderer, she pressed herself against the wall as though she was afraid of him even brushing past her.

Vallier entered the hallway.

The lounge door was open.

Yvonne, sitting on an armchair, was weeping, while Monsieur Aubry offered the most affectionate consolations.

"Mademoiselle Yvonne," began the Lieutenant. "I wanted to express to you…"

But, incapable of overcoming the indignation that was gnawing away inside him, he cried out, "Oh! The wretches! If you knew... if you only knew!"

The orphan raised her head.

"My love, what is it?" she asked, flummoxed by the sight of her fiancé whose features were expressing the most noble rage.

Then, his willpower and patience exhausted, the Lieutenant burst out, "I've been accused of being your father's murderer."

"You…" the young girl gave a start of dread.

"You!" repeated Monsieur Aubry, no less terrified than the Colonel's daughter.

"Yes, me! Me!" the innocent man exclaimed.

"But, that's mad! That's insane!" Yvonne replied with a voice that betrayed endless distress.

"I beg your pardon for having caused you still more sorrow," replied Vallier. "But, on seeing you, I was unable to contain myself. I didn't want you to learn of this from another. It's so shocking!"

"Be calm, and tell us what happened," the inventor advised, having regained his composure.

Trying to master his emotions too, Raymond Vallier explained.

"At the cemetery, as soon as you left with Monsieur Aubry, something unheard-of happened. This time, it was no longer insinuations, mutterings, noises, gossip, which had already reached my ears, and which I had rejected with disdain... but a clear, brutal direct accusation. Yes, they treated me as though I was the murderer!

"And do you know who gave the signal? Gerfaut... the factory's best worker, whose influence over his colleagues is considerable! Mademoiselle Yvonne, they were all yelling that I killed your father!"

A clamour could suddenly be heard in front of the powder mill.

Then the young officer, waving his fist in the direction from which the shouts were coming, cried out in a strong voice. "Ah! The madmen! The wretches!"

While the shouting doubled in volume, Yvonne, without saying a word, but with a decisive gesture, leapt towards the window, her eyes haggard, her mouth pinched, her chest heaving.

"What are you going to do?" asked Jean Aubry, who had followed her.

Pointing to the crowd which was beginning to gather behind the powder mill gates, the Colonel's daughter cried out, in a voice filled with indomitable energy:

"Proclaim his innocence to them! Proclaim to them that they're mistaken, that it wasn't Lieutenant Vallier who killed my father, that it couldn't have been him..."

But suddenly, she stopped.

A cry of distress was choked in her throat. "The police!"

It was them, indeed, who were forcing the increasingly exalted workers to clear the powder mill entrance and to make way for a gentleman dressed in a black frock coat and a top hat.

He, crossing the entrance, headed immediately towards the Richard house, followed by two representatives of the authorities.

In the house's small lounge, a tragic silence now reigned.

They distinctly heard the footsteps of the magistrate and the two gendarmes, crunching through the gravel in the garden, then hammering on the granite steps before finally echoing on the hallway flagstones.

A dark silhouette appeared at the threshold, asking in a clipped, incisive voice, "Lieutenant Raymond Vallier?"

"That's me, Monsieur," replied the officer, taking a step forward.

"Lieutenant, I'm the Police Commissioner: furnished with a warrant to search…"

Jean Aubry intervened. "You could have at least waited a few hours before subjecting Mademoiselle Richard to this fresh ordeal."

"I have orders!" the Commissioner replied drily.

And addressing Vallier, he said in an imperious tone, "Take me immediately to your private quarters."

The officer made as if to obey the Commissioner.

But Yvonne, who could barely contain herself, cried out. "I suppose there's no intention of giving credence to the odious lies that are being circulated at present."

The representative of the law looked at the young girl with an expression of sad compassion. "Mademoiselle," he said, "this is very painful, but I must carry out my mission. It will suffer no delay. I repeat, I am very sorry."

And turning back, he added, "Lieutenant, I must ask you to follow me."

"In that case, Monsieur, I'll accompany you." Mademoiselle Richard's voice was admirably firm.

And turning to Monsieur Aubry, she added, "Come, you too, dear Monsieur Aubry, because I insist that the truth be brought out into the cold light of day!"

25 WHERE CRIME PREVAILS…

The Police Commissioner and Raymond Vallier were first to leave the house.

Yvonne and the inventor followed them a few steps behind, preceding the two gendarmes who must have received instructions not to let the officer out of their sight for a single minute.

He, sure of himself, admirably brave in the face of danger, led the magistrate to his quarters, where they all entered, including the gendarmes.

"Here are my keys," said Yvonne's fiancé, holding out a keyring to the commissioner who, instead of taking them, first looked hard at Raymond Vallier.

"Do you have a revolver?" he asked in the same imperious tone.

"Yes, Monsieur."

"Well then! Give it to me."

Vallier went straight to the nightstand drawer, opened it, and took out the weapon… a standard issue revolver which was found right at the bottom of the furniture.

He held it out to the commissioner, saying, "Here you are, Monsieur."

The lawman took it and, before examining it, asked, "Is it loaded?"

"Yes, Monsieur."

"How many rounds?"

"Six."

"We shall see."

The commissioner opened the barrel.

After casting a quick glance at it, he added, "Has it been long since you used this weapon?"

"About a month. I took a few practice shots."

"And you're sure that this weapon indeed contained six live rounds?"

"I'm all the surer as it was I who reloaded it."

"Well, you're lying!"

"I'm lying!"

"Yes, see for yourself. Of the six rounds, two of them are spent. See those empty cartridges, that you didn't even take the trouble to remove!"

And in a theatrical tone, the magistrate declared, "I'm doubtless telling you nothing you didn't know. But I must inform you that this revolver is of the same calibre as that which was used to kill Colonel Richard."

With a satisfied and sardonic air, the commissioner added, "A simple passing observation. Now, take me to your office."

"First," replied Vallier, "I must affirm that I've not used this revolver since…"

"Take me to your office!" the magistrate insisted in a commanding tone which was almost menacing.

By a path which led from the engineer's lodging to the administrative building, the little procession, still followed by the two gendarmes, reached the office.

In the distance, the crowd was still grumbling.

Vallier felt himself struck by inexpressible anguish.

"Those two missing bullets," he thought, "are becoming peculiarly strange and disquieting. And yet, I'm sure, I loaded my gun myself, and I've not touched it since. What does this mean?"

When he pushed the door to his office open to admit the police commissioner, he was beginning to wonder whether he might be dreaming, or if he was the victim of the most dreadful stitch-up that had ever been dreamed up against an honest man.

This time, the magistrate seized the keys that, mechanically, Yvonne's fiancé held out to him, and he began the search, rummaging in the drawers, not leaving a single file without having leafed through it compulsively, and all amid the increasingly tragic silence of the witnesses, a silence broken from time to time by the shouts of the mob which echoed in the distance.

Suddenly, the magistrate stopped, visibly moved.

He had just discovered, at the bottom of a cardboard box, a bundle of documents, sealed in a large yellow envelope which he had immediately opened.

Hardly had he glanced through the contents when he let out a cry of triumph.

"This time, it's definitive. Here at last is the proof, undeniable, unarguable, absolute."

And, turning to Raymond Vallier in one brusque movement, he declared, putting his hand on the Lieutenant's shoulder:

"In the name of the law, I'm arresting you, under the double charge of the murder of Monsieur Richard and of high treason towards your country!"

"Me, a traitor! Me, a murderer!" the young officer shouted. "It's a lie, I swear to you. I'm a victim of the most odious machinations. I'm innocent! Innocent, do you hear me! In arresting me, commissioner, you're committing the most dreadful judicial error."

"Silence!"

"No! I will not be silent! I won't have enough strength and energy to protest against the dishonourable trick of which I'm the victim. But I'm at peace! It won't be long before I emerge from this ordeal, my head held high. And you, Commissioner, will be obliged to apologise to the French officer whose uniform you're about to drag through the mud, on the word of gossips…"

"Gossips!"

"Yes, Commissioner, gossips, and perhaps some vague coincidences whose fragility can't have eluded you."

"We shall see," retorted the magistrate gravely, seeming in no way disposed to let himself be circumvented.

And he added, "Follow me!"

Then he made a swift gesture.

The gendarmes, who had been standing slightly apart, stepped forward at once and as one of them took a pair of handcuffs from his pocket, Yvonne Richard who, one moment, had felt herself flagging, immediately regained all her strength, and rushing between her fiancé and the representatives of the law, she cried out in a desperate voice.

"Stop… stop! He's innocent, I'm sure of it. Absolutely innocent! Yes, yes, he's innocent!"

"You have proof of that?" the Commissioner asked with a sceptical air.

"Proof, oh yes," the young girl replied. "I find it first in my conviction that Lieutenant Vallier is incapable of such a vile act. And why would he kill my father? Why would he betray him?"

"Yes, why?" Raymond repeated, stimulated by the aid brought to him by the woman he loved, galvanised by the unshakeable faith in him that Yvonne demonstrated.

Sure of himself, mastering the indignation which galvanised his nerves, he continued.

"Now that Colonel Richard is dead, I can speak. I can defend myself, because I'm sure that if he was still alive, and saw me accused of such a dreadful double crime, he would be the first to release me from the oath he imposed on me."

"What oath?" the Commissioner asked in an incredulous tone.

"On the night of the 4th of June, you hear me, Commissioner, I'm precise… on the night of the 4th of June, having noticed a light in my commanding officer's office, I reported to him immediately… and to my stupefaction and joy, I found myself face to face with Colonel Richard.

"Ah! I knew it!" Yvonne interrupted, shivering.

But Jean Aubry who, throughout this tragic scene, hadn't ceased to maintain the most marvellous composure, whispered in the orphan's ear.

"Let him speak. I'll intervene myself, when the time is right."

The Lieutenant continued. "As I expressed to my Colonel how happy I was to see him again, he made me give my word of honour not to reveal to anyone, even and particularly his daughter, that he had returned to the powder mill."

Vallier was about to continue his tale, but the commissioner interrupted him. "You're really saying that on the night of the 4th of June, you saw Colonel Richard in his office?"

"Precisely, Monsieur."

"So, you're lying again."

"I'm lying!"

"The report from medical experts established in a peremptory fashion that the Colonel was murdered before the date you're invoking for your defence."

"The doctors are mistaken," Yvonne declared energetically. "Because I too, I can testify that I also saw father on the night that Monsieur Vallier is invoking."

"Come, Mademoiselle," the magistrate replied with a certain severity, "don't try to save your father's murderer… and allow me to be astonished that, with the evidence piled against him, I find you, alone perhaps, defending him."

"Alone, no," Jean Aubry said in turn. "Because I too am convinced of his innocence."

As events were unfolding, wheels were turning in the inventor's mind.

He recalled, not only that Chantecoq had declared to him, without giving any other details, his faith in the officer's absolute innocence.

And he thought, "For Chantecoq to have affirmed his conviction in such a categorical fashion, he must possess some first-rate arguments, and perhaps even decisive evidence."

And, remembering also that he had seen the detective wearing Richard's features in Avenue Trudaine, he deduced logically that he might very well have used this subterfuge in

Douai just as easily as in Paris. And that there lay one of the keys to the mystery.

So he continued with a tone of the most obvious conviction. "In this terrible business, there has been, I'm sure, a dreadful misunderstanding!"

"But first, Monsieur!" the Commissioner cut in. "Who are you, to permit yourself to intervene in this case like this?"

"I'm Monsieur Jean Aubry," the great scholar said simply.

"Jean Aubry!" the magistrate repeated, as though he was unaware of the name, which was so illustrious throughout the world.

"The inventor of the combat aircraft," Germaine's father felt he ought to qualify himself.

"Ah! Yes, very good," snapped the representative of the law, a little irritated at being caught out in such a flagrant piece of ignorance.

And at once, with a courtesy that was more exterior than genuine, he went on. "Permit me, Monsieur, to be astonished that a personality of your intelligence and character, would reason so strangely when faced with such evidence."

"Evidence!" Jean Aubry repeated.

"Everything points to this man," declared the magistrate, pointing at Vallier with a vengeful finger. "It's not for me to discuss with him the facts which implicate him. But, as at present, I defy him to explain to me, after having affirmed before you that he's not used his gun for several months, why his revolver is missing two bullets which are of exactly the same calibre as those which served to kill Colonel Richard. I believe this is more than a vague coincidence."

As Raymond Vallier raised his hands in protest, the Police Commissioner said at once, showing him the papers that he was holding, "And these documents?"

"What documents?" the Lieutenant cried.

"Ah! Come on," replied the magistrate, "don't play ignorant."

"I swear to you I have no idea what they contain."

"Come off it, they're in your handwriting and they establish your links with a foreign power."

"In that case, they're fake," Vallier protested.

"Experts will establish that," the Commissioner replied. "Meanwhile, I have a duty to consider them to be authentic. Anyway, it's enough to browse through quickly to understand that they establish a very direct correlation between your treachery and Colonel Richard's murder."

"I protest in the strongest possible terms," Yvonne's fiancé tried to shout.

But this time it was Jean Aubry who intervened. "I think I already know a fair few things," he declared. "I propose to reveal to the prosecutor, to him alone, because this consists of secrets relevant to national defence and Lieutenant Vallier will be the first to understand that I'm constrained to exercise the greatest prudence."

"Certainly," the Lieutenant agreed. "I'm one of those ready to make any sacrifice when it's a question of protecting the Fatherland!"

"Thank you, I'm glad, Lieutenant. Not only do I firmly believe in your innocence, but I'm convinced that it won't take long to be recognised. So I deplore…"

A violent clamour interrupted the scholar.

"You hear them," the Police Commissioner said simply. "If I don't act immediately, those people are so over-excited that they're capable of overcoming our men, taking our prisoner from us and doing him an ill turn. The best thing to do then, in everyone's interests, is to get this over with as quickly as possible."

"So be it! Monsieur," Vallier said, "take me away. It would be best, indeed."

"Raymond…" Yvonne tried to express herself, sobbing.

"Don't worry," the officer declared firmly. "I shall unmask my enemies and I'll return to you soon, to resume my post of honour and combat. Yes, it's with a glad heart and a clean conscience that I entrust you to the admirable Monsieur Jean Aubry, and that I bid you *au revoir,* and that I'll see you soon."

"See you soon," repeated the young girl, holding out her hand to her fiancé who seized it and brought it respectfully to his lips.

Then turning back to the magistrate, Vallier spoke to him in a curt, decisive voice.

"Now, Monsieur, I'm at your disposal."

"Bravo!" Jean Aubry applauded. "There indeed is the attitude of an innocent man."

And, going straight to the magistrate, whom he enveloped in his penetrating gaze, he said, superb in his dignity and strength, he said, "Monsieur Police Commissioner, whatever charges that a criminal hand was able to accumulate against this young man, after having made me his guarantor, I'll see you in court.

"You'll be the first then to regret such a frightful error and to proclaim before the world that not only is Lieutenant Raymond Vallier no murderer or traitor, but that he deserves respect from everyone!"

The magistrate, speechless, bowed with a politeness which retained a certain measure of reserve.

Then, at his signal, the gendarmes, more impressed than they wanted to show, surrounded the prisoner who, strengthened by the faith of his fiancée, of Jean Aubry, and of General Framer, seemed resigned to his fate.

Then, the Commissioner opened the door and ventured outside, followed by the captive and his guards, while a storm of imprecations, furious threats and screams of blue murder raged.

"Death! Death to the murderer!"

Adjusting his tricolore scarf, the representative of the law went towards the crowd.

"My friends," he said, "I recommend the most absolute calm. Instead of impeding the work of justice, instead show yourself to be its precious auxiliaries, by not stooping to any disagreeable displays against this prisoner, for whom I am responsible."

Those words, pronounced in a fashion that was pompous and stertorous, had the result of shutting up the majority of the loudmouths.

But, as the most turbulent were persisting and as some menacing fists were still waving, the magistrate ordered, "Gendarmes, draw your swords, and clear a path."

This time, order was restored.

The Police Commissioner, showing his prisoner into the car which had brought him, sat next to Vallier, while the two gendarmes sat opposite him and a brigadier climbed up next to the driver.

The car set off quite slowly, parting the ranks of the mob, who made way before the vehicle, all the time murmuring and making vague threatening gestures, tempered immediately by the sight of the swords glittering in the sunlight.

Then, having passed through the barrier, the car set off at top speed in the direction of Douai, while, from the window of her house, Yvonne Richard, struck in the heart twice, sent the most sublime kisses towards the captive, then fell back into the arms of Jean Aubry, now her sole protector in the world.

Then, an old beggar woman, who was standing some distance away, approached Gerfaut, who had not ceased stimulating the unthinking rage of the workers who had been cleverly stirred up by him. She whispered in his ear.

"Until this evening, yes? Because we still have work to do."

"Until this evening," repeated the bandit, while Wilhelm's spy lost herself in the crowd.

**TO BE CONTINUED IN
CHANTECOQ AND WILHELM'S SPY VOL.2
THE ENEMY WITHIN!**

ABOUT THE AUTHOR

Arthur Bernède (5 January 1871 – 20 March 1937) was a
French writer, poet, opera librettist, and playwright.

Bernède was born in Redon, Ille-et-Vilaine department, in
Brittany. In 1919, Bernède joined forces with actor René
Navarre, who had played Fantômas in the Louis Feuillade
serials, and writer Gaston Leroux, the creator of Rouletabille,
to launch the Société des Cinéromans, a production company
that would produce films and novels simultaneously. Bernède
published almost 200 adventure, mystery, and historical
novels. His best-known characters are Belphégor, Judex,
Mandrin, Chantecoq, and Vidocq. Bernède also collaborated
on plays, poems, and opera libretti with Paul de Choudens;
including several operas by Félix Fourdrain.

Bernède also wrote the libretti for a number of operas,
among them Jules Massenet's Sapho and Camille Erlanger's
L'Aube rouge.

ABOUT THE TRANSLATOR

Andrew Lawston grew up in rural Hampshire, where he later
worked for a short time as a French teacher. He moved to
London to work in magazine publishing, alongside pursuing
his interests in writing, translation, and acting.

In addition to translating the chronicles of Chantecoq for the
English-speaking world, Andrew has written a number of
science-fiction and urban fantasy books, full of his particular
brand of humour. Andrew currently lives in West London
with his lovely wife Mel, and a little black cat called Buscemi.
There, he cooks curries, enjoys beer and quality cinema, and
he dreams of a better world.

ALSO AVAILABLE

CHANTECOQ

Chantecoq and the Aubry Affair
Chantecoq and Wilhelm's Spy I: Made In Germany
Chantecoq and Wilhelm's Spy II: The Enemy Within
Chantecoq and Wilhelm's Spy III: The Day of Reckoning
Chantecoq and the Mystery of the Blue Train
Chantecoq and the Haunted House
Chantecoq and the Aviator's Crime
Chantecoq and Zapata
Chantecoq and the Amorous Ogre
Chantecoq and the Père-Lachaise Ghost
Chantecoq and the Condemned Woman
Chantecoq and the Ladykiller
Chantecoq and the Devil's Daughter

By Andrew Lawston
Detective Daintypaws: A Squirrel in Bohemia
Detective Daintypaws: Buscemi at Christmas
Detective Daintypaws: Murder on the Tesco Express
Zip! Zap! Boing!
Voyage of the Space Bastard
Rudy on Rails

Printed in Great Britain
by Amazon

11655424R00123